"My father is matchmaking."

Harry looked puzzled. "Why would he do that?"

"He wants me to stay in Rawhide," Melissa explained. "He's trying to find someone to marry me."

The deputy grinned and raised his brows. "That shouldn't be too difficult."

"If that's a compliment, thank you. But I don't think you understand that Dad has chosen *you* as the primary candidate for my not-so-future husband. You'd better start running."

"Assuming I'm not interested."

Her voice was firm when she told him, "It doesn't matter. I'm going back to Paris after the holidays."

"Oh, yeah? Then I'd better kiss you goodbye."

Without any more warning, he pulled her into his arms and planted a kiss on her lips like none she'd ever received. Then he walked away, leaving her befuddled brain to wonder—if that was a goodbye peck, what would his real kiss be like?

Dear Reader,

Welcome, once again, to Rawhide, Wyoming, the home of the Randalls. This is the story of Griff and Camille's (*Cowboy Come Home*) daughter. Melissa left home six years ago to study in France and hasn't been back since. When her mother asks her to come home for the holidays as a present to her, Melissa agrees. Then the magic of Rawhide, and all her family, wraps around Melissa and persuades her to return to the fold.

Of course, there's also Deputy Sheriff Harry Gowan, who was introduced in *A Randall Returns.* He is the perfect match for Melissa—at least he appears to be, until a visitor from France arrives on the scene. Then confusion reigns!

I really love writing the Randalls—they make me feel as if I've come home again. I hope you enjoy this book, and look forward to our next visit to Rawhide, Wyoming, and the Randall family.

And here's to Thanksgiving, a time for family and gratefulness. What better holiday to celebrate with the Randalls!

Judy Christenberry

A RANDALL THANKSGIVING

Judy Christenberry

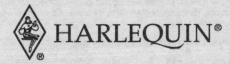

HARLEQUIN®

TORONTO • NEW YORK • LONDON
AMSTERDAM • PARIS • SYDNEY • HAMBURG
STOCKHOLM • ATHENS • TOKYO • MILAN • MADRID
PRAGUE • WARSAW • BUDAPEST • AUCKLAND

ISBN-13: 978-0-373-75137-2
ISBN-10:   0-373-75137-0

A RANDALL THANKSGIVING

www.eHarlequin.com

Printed in U.S.A.

ABOUT THE AUTHOR

Judy Christenberry has been writing romances for over fifteen years because she loves happy endings as much as her readers do. A former French teacher, Judy now devotes herself to writing full-time. She hopes readers have as much fun with her stories as she does. She spends her spare time reading, watching her favorite sports teams and keeping track of her two daughters. Judy lives in Texas.

Books by Judy Christenberry

HARLEQUIN AMERICAN ROMANCE

*Brides for Brothers
†Tots for Texans
**Children of Texas

Chapter One

From under his hat, Deputy Sheriff Harry Gowan surveyed the scene at the local steak house and bar in Rawhide, Wyoming. It was Friday, the second busiest night in town. And he was in charge of keeping the peace.

His roving gaze stopped when it lit on a young woman sitting at a table in the center of the room. She didn't look like an inhabitant of Rawhide, with her short, spiky brown hair and that bright red lipstick on her pouty lips. Still, she was beautiful…and she was alone.

He strolled over to her table. He had no objection to strangers in his town, and besides, as an employee of the city, wasn't it part of his job to make people feel at home in Rawhide?

"Evening, ma'am," he said, tipping his hat. "I suspect you might be new to town. If there's anything I can do to help you enjoy your stay, please let me know."

The young woman smiled at him and he was struck by her beautiful blue eyes.

"How nice of you. I could use a dance partner," she said, looking expectantly at him.

Now Harry was embarrassed. He fought the urge to back away. "Sorry, ma'am, but I can't dance with you."

"Why not…Sheriff?" she ventured.

"Deputy," he clarified, nodding at the badge on his chest. "I'm on duty, and dancing isn't in the deputy manual. The sheriff would fire me if he caught me. Besides, I'm a really lousy dancer," he confessed. "But I can get you a partner."

Without waiting for her consent, he turned and headed for the bar, where a few cowboys had their boots propped up on the foot rail. "Hey, Josh," he called out to a friend. "I've got a favor to ask."

"Anything, buddy."

"There's this knockout looking for a dance partner. I told her I'd find her one."

Josh broke into a smile. "Lead the way. I haven't met a real knockout in a while." He put down his beer and followed Harry across the room. "Where is she?"

"Right there," Harry said, pointing toward the center table.

Josh came to an abrupt halt. "Wait a minute. You don't mean that siren sitting by herself, do you?"

Harry let himself look at the woman. "Who else? She's something, isn't she?"

"Yeah, she's something, all right, but I won't be dancing with her."

Harry stared at his friend as if he'd lost his mind. "Why not?"

"'Cause I don't dance with my cousins, Harry."

"Cousin?"

"People would think I was crazy…or weird."

"She's a Randall?" Harry stared at the woman. "No, she can't be. I know all the Randalls!"

"She's been living in France since before you came to Rawhide. She's Uncle Griff's daughter."

"What are we going to do? I promised to find her a partner."

Josh surveyed the room. "There's Dwight Barnes. He's a dancer."

"Yeah, but…" Barnes wouldn't be Harry's first choice but he'd do. "Okay, you go get him while I tell her he's coming."

Harry walked back to the table where the young lady sat sipping a beer. "I didn't know you were a Randall."

"Aren't Randalls allowed to dance?" she asked, her eyes teasing.

He bit back Josh's retort, saying instead, "Your cousin Josh went to get a guy to dance with you—Dwight Barnes. I just wanted to tell you not to go outside alone with him." When she seemed taken aback by his warning, he hurriedly said, "Dwight's a good dancer, but… Well, you don't know him, so I thought I should say something."

"Thanks for the warning, Deputy," she said sweetly, "but I do know how to handle men."

"Then my apologies," Harry said, and tipped his hat, prepared to walk away.

"Wait," she said at once. "You haven't told me your name." She fluttered her thick lashes at him.

"I'm Harry Gowan, deputy sheriff."

"Nice to meet you, Harry Gowan, deputy sheriff." She flashed him a brilliant white smile, momentarily stunning him. He was about to ask her name when Josh strode up, the dancer cowboy following.

"Hey, Melissa, this is Dwight Barnes."

"How nice to meet you, Mr. Barnes," Melissa said.

Harry watched her flutter those same lashes at Barnes and was pleased to see that he wasn't the only man who melted at her feet.

He guessed Ms. Randall was telling the truth. She did know how to handle men.

MELISSA RANDALL RETURNED to her parents' house at 11:00 p.m., an incredibly early hour if she were still in Paris. It was even early in Rawhide, Wyoming, on the weekend.

Her parents were waiting up for her, making her feel more like an eighteen-year-old than a twenty-six-year-old who had lived abroad for six years.

"Hello, dear," her mother said with a smile. "Did you have fun?"

Melissa debated how to answer that question. She loved her mother dearly and didn't want to hurt her feelings, but Paris was so much more exciting than Rawhide. "Uh, yeah, it was all right."

Griff Randall eyed his daughter a bit sharply. "Did you meet anyone new?"

"Dwight Barnes."

"Dwight Barnes?" he blustered. "You need to keep away from him!"

"I know," Melissa said.

Her mother frowned. "What do you mean by that? Did he do something he shouldn't have?"

"No, but the deputy sheriff warned me about him."

"Which deputy sheriff?" her father demanded.

"You mean Rawhide has more than one?" Melissa asked in mock awe.

"That's enough of that, young lady," he retorted. "Now tell me his name."

"Harry Gooden, I think."

"And I think that would be Harry Gowan."

"Oh. Well, I was close."

"I'm sure he'll appreciate that," her father said, letting his sarcasm show.

"Dad!" Melissa protested, dragging the word out as a teenager would do.

"And here I thought our daughter had grown up."

"Griff, you're being too hard on her. She just got back the other night. She probably still has jet lag," her mother protested.

"That's her own damn fault, Camille. She lives too far away from home. This is her first visit in six years!"

"But you and Mom came to see me. Wasn't that fun?"

"It was for me, sweetheart," her mother immediately said. "But these past four years have seemed like forever."

"I know, Mom, and I intended to come home before now, but—but I got busy and—"

"And then there was Pierre," Griff growled.

"You told me you liked him!" Melissa protested.

"That was before I knew he was your lover!"

"Dad!"

"Griff!" Camille protested at the same time. Before Melissa could say anything else, her mother added, "You promised, Griff."

"I know, but she asked!"

"Both of you, go to bed. I can't handle the arguments this late at night!" Camille said in exasperation.

Both father and daughter, so much alike, immediately said they were sorry. Camille accepted their apologies but insisted she was heading to bed, and Griff immediately agreed to join her. They both kissed their daughter good-night and left the kitchen together.

Melissa stood there, thinking about one of the things she'd missed in her glamorous life in Paris. It was seeing how much her parents loved each other and remained faithful to one another no matter what.

She didn't know any older married couples in France. Still, she was pretty sure that a marriage like her parents' wasn't normal anywhere. Her father wasn't about to let his wife go to bed without him, especially when he was afraid she was still a little mad at him.

Melissa found a smile on her lips and warmth in her heart as she thought about her parents' love affair. Even while growing up, she'd noticed their devotion to each other. She'd never had any doubt about their faithfulness. As an adult, she realized how unusual it was, though she knew her dad would just tell her it was a Randall trait.

Melissa really wasn't sleepy, but she strolled to the room that had been hers before she'd gone to France. The move had been a hard-fought battle, one she hadn't thought she could win. She couldn't have without her mom's backing. But Melissa had done so well in French in her first two years of college that her professor had helped convince her mother to let her live in France for one semester.

And she'd never come home.

Until now.

When she'd asked her mom what she'd like for Christmas, her mother had simply said, "For you to come home for the holidays."

Melissa couldn't say no to her. Camille was such a sweet, gentle person. But she was also a fighter. When she realized how much Melissa had wanted to go to France, she'd fought hard for Griff's approval. There had been several days when Camille wouldn't even speak to her husband.

Melissa owed her mother big time.

HARRY WAS PUMPING IRON, his muscles straining under the two-hundred-pound bar. He'd just finished a half hour on the treadmill, set at a steep incline, and he was still sweating. But he needed it. The workout center had been added on to the Sheriff's Office several years ago. When Mike Davis had become sheriff, he'd wanted his men to be in good physical shape so that using a firearm was not their first thought when subduing a lawbreaker.

Mike had asked the Randalls if they could get together with other ranchers in the area to contribute a modest sum for a couple of weight machines. The Randalls, who never did anything in a small way, had showed up at his door the next morning to begin remodeling the storeroom into a first-rate workout facility.

In gratitude, Mike had opened the facility to all the men in town as long as his staff had dibs at certain times of the day. Right now only Harry and his partner, Steve Lawson, were working out, spotting each other.

Harry had just returned the heavy bar to its stand and sat up, sweat dripping from his brow, when a sweet voice asked from the doorway, "Is Harry Gowan in here?"

Steve whirled around, almost losing his balance. "Lady, this is a men's facility. You can't come in here!"

With a pouty smile that Harry recognized at once, Melissa Randall said, "Well, technically, I haven't come into the room. Oh, hi, Harry," she said, her smile widening as she saw him turn to face her.

Harry was wearing a pair of shorts and nothing else.

Now he wished he had a T-shirt or a towel nearby so he could cover up a little. "Hello, Melissa. I'm afraid I'm not dressed for company. If you'll give me a minute, I'll be right out."

"Oh, I don't mind," she said, her smile increasing as she took in the sight of his muscled chest.

"Yeah, but I do. I'll be right with you."

Conceding gracefully, Melissa fluttered her fingers in a wave as she stepped back and let the door shut again.

Steve stared at his partner. "Who was that? I've never seen her before."

"I hadn't either until last night," Harry said, grabbing a towel and drying himself off.

"You must've had a good night."

"Not like you're thinking. I just met her, that's all."

"Yeah, right."

"I meant it, Steve, and I'd better not hear you spreading any gossip about her." Harry added a glare to convince his partner.

The man backed away. "I wouldn't, Harry, I promise, but she is really hot."

"Yeah, she's also a Randall." He pulled on his sweat pants.

"A Randall? I thought I knew all the Randalls by now."

"She's been living in France for the past six years." He belted his gun holster at the small of his back and pulled on a sweatshirt that covered it.

Steve was still standing there with his mouth open.

"What's the matter? You've never heard of France?" Harry teased.

"I've never heard of a Randall being in France," Steve replied.

"Me, neither, but I guess wonders never cease."

MELISSA WAS SEATED AT ONE of the empty desks close to the workout facility. When she heard the door open, she spun around, eager to get another look at Harry Gowan. Unfortunately, he'd put on a sweatshirt that covered up that impressive chest.

"I hope I didn't embarrass you," she said, though she wasn't being truthful by any means.

Much to her surprise, Harry said, "Yeah, I could tell that was weighing on your mind." He sounded just like her dad when he was being sarcastic.

Narrowing her eyes, she smiled and held up a box. "I brought you something." That should make him feel bad about being sarcastic!

"Why?"

Melissa stiffened. What was wrong with the man? He should've been falling all over himself, apologizing. "Because my daddy said I owed you something for trying to warn me about Dwight Barnes."

"You didn't seem to appreciate it last night."

Now she was really getting irritated. "This was my father's idea!" she exclaimed, and shoved the box toward him.

"I can't accept payment," he said calmly.

Melissa felt steam blowing out her ears. She nailed him in his rock-hard stomach with the box. "It's a damn box of cookies. I don't care what you do with it!" And she stomped out of the office.

When she reached the sidewalk, she regretted her loss of control, but it was too late to do anything about it now. She just hoped her father didn't come to town and run into Harry. She'd never hear the end of it.

Since her cousins' accounting office was just across the street, Melissa went over there to see if Tori wanted to go to lunch. At least someone in Rawhide would treat her nicely.

Tori agreed to go as soon as Russ got back. He usually went home for lunch, Tori explained, since he and his wife had had a second child, a little boy.

"I'm looking forward to Sunday dinner so I can meet everyone who's new to the family," Melissa said.

"There's a fair number," Tori replied. "Including my latest."

"Another baby? How many have you had?"

"Just three. And he may be my last."

"You sound kind of sad about that," Melissa noted. "I thought you intended to be a career woman."

"I did. But Jon…well, he was just too hard to resist." She laughed. "Men can be like that, you know."

"I think I do."

"I bet you just bat your lashes and they fall to their knees all around you."

"Not exactly," Melissa replied darkly.

Tori's eyebrows soared. "Oh? Was it in France or here in Rawhide?"

"Here, and it's no big deal. I think Dad was trying to play matchmaker like Uncle Jake."

"And you went along with it?"

"Yeah. The guy was kind of cute and I thought I might enjoy my trip more if I had someone to go out with. I'm only going to be here for about six weeks."

"And he wasn't interested? The man must be made out of stone…or married. You wouldn't try to date a married man, would you, Melissa? I mean, I know that some people are different about things like that, but it wouldn't— I mean, here in Rawhide, it's not—"

Before Tori could try again to explain the mores in Rawhide, Melissa told her, "Remember, I said my dad had set me up? I don't think he'd choose a married man for me."

"Oh, right, of course."

"And just for the record, I wouldn't go for a married man, either, here or in France."

"I'm sorry for even thinking that, Melissa, but you've been gone so long and the French—"

"I know. But I'm a Randall, not a Frenchman."

Tori smiled. "Good. So who gave you a hard time?"

"You probably don't know him."

"In Rawhide? You've got to be kidding."

"Okay, it was Harry Gowan."

"Harry? Harry was mean to you?" Tori asked in disbelief.

"I didn't say he was mean. He was just…disinterested."

"He must be going blind, honey. You're beautiful, what with that hairstyle and your makeup."

"Am I wearing too much makeup?"

"No. I keep staring at your eyes. They look so natural but they stand out. I'm impressed."

"It's because I got Mom's blue eyes with Dad's hair color. Around here, all the Randalls seem to be brown-eyed."

"You've got a point there. But Jess and I don't look like regular Randalls, either," said the blond, blue-eyed Tori.

"I know. I always liked that about you two. How is Jessica?"

"She's due any day now."

"More babies? I'll never keep them straight!"

"Yes, you will. Give it time. Just remember, we're all family."

As if on cue, the door opened and Russ entered the outer office.

"Hey, Russ," Melissa said, hugging her cousin. "I haven't seen you in six years. Looks like fatherhood agrees with you."

He gave her a kiss on the cheek. "You've certainly grown up."

"Thank you, kind sir."

"Where are you two headed?" he asked as Melissa and Tori walked toward the door.

"We're going over to the café for lunch," Tori said.

"I think I'll join you. I can have a piece of pie while y'all eat your lunch."

"I thought one of us was going to stay at the office all the time. Isn't that what we decided?" Tori asked.

"Yeah, but today's a special occasion." He winked at Melissa. "I'll just tell Cora to call my cell if something comes up."

"Be quick about it," Tori said. "We're both starving."

A few seconds later Russ held open the door, and the two women went out. They'd reached the other side of the street when, behind them, they heard Russ greet someone.

"Why don't you join us? I'll buy you a piece of pie," Russ called out.

The women turned around, and that was when Melissa came face-to-face with the living, breathing cause of her irritation.

Harry Gowan.

Chapter Two

Melissa held her breath as she waited for Harry's answer. It confused her that she didn't even know what she wanted most—for him to accept the invitation or to reject it.

"Thanks, Russ, but I'm on duty. Mike frowns on me spending all my time in the café." He added a smile, which was more than he'd done for her.

"I understand. But let me introduce my long lost cousin Melissa, Griff and Camille's daughter. She's been living in France."

Without looking her way, he replied, "I met her last night. She seems to be adjusting well."

Melissa stomped her foot. "Quit talking about me like I'm not here!"

He finally looked at her. "Certainly, Miss Randall." Then he quickly averted his gaze. "See you 'round, Russ, Tori." And he walked away.

Tori and Russ stared after him, and looked at Melissa.

"What?" she demanded, feeling defensive.

Russ said, "Let's get our table. Then we'll talk."

Once they were seated and had gotten their coffee and given their orders, Russ turned to Melissa. "You've only been here a few days. How have you managed to upset one of the nicest guys in town?"

"Are you referring to Harry Gowan?" Melissa demanded. "Because he hasn't been so nice to me!"

Russ glanced at Tori. "What's going on? Are they already involved?"

"No!" Melissa nearly spat out her coffee.

Tori put a calming hand on her arm, then explained, "It's another case of a father matchmaking for his daughter, a Randall pastime, you know. And apparently, though I find it hard to believe, Harry wasn't interested."

Russ shifted his gaze to Melissa. "I'm surprised. I figured guys would be lined up for the opportunity to get close to you, Melissa."

"Thank you, but apparently I only appeal to men with loose morals," she said glumly.

"Who in particular?" Russ asked sternly.

She rolled her eyes. "You're as bad as Harry."

"Wait a minute. I'm getting confused. Where does Harry come in?"

Melissa sighed. "Harry warned me last night not to go outside with Dwight Barnes. And Dad said I should bake him some cookies to say thank you. So I did, because I wanted to please Dad. But Harry wouldn't even take the cookies."

"What did you do with them?" Russ asked.

"I hit him in the stomach with the box and walked

out. I don't know what he did with them after that. Probably threw them in the trash!"

"Oh, my," Tori said softly.

"It wasn't my fault. I did what Dad asked."

"I guess you did. But just a word of warning," Russ said with a smile. "Harry is a favorite with the family and he's frequently invited to Sunday dinner."

Moaning, Melissa buried her face in her hands. "I'm doomed. Dad's going to be upset with me and that will upset Mom and—and—"

"I know," Tori said, patting Melissa's shoulder. "No one ever wants to upset Camille. She's so sweet."

Melissa nodded. "She's the one who convinced Dad to let me go to France. It wasn't easy. She even stopped speaking to him for several days."

"I didn't know that," Tori said. "I wondered why Uncle Griff let you go at such a young age. But it was only supposed to be for a semester, wasn't it?"

"Yes, until one of the greatest jewelry designers in the world looked at my work and offered me a chance to learn from him. It was an incredible offer I had to accept."

"Did you make those?" Tori asked, reaching out to touch the twisted gold earrings Melissa was wearing.

"Yes. Monsieur Jalbert is letting me design some more casual jewelry, different from the expensive, heavy pieces that you'd only wear at balls or galas."

"Of which we have none," Russ commented. "But I have heard of the man. My wife used to buy that kind of jewelry, before she moved to Rawhide."

"Did you bring any other pieces with you?" Tori asked, still staring at the earrings. "I don't know how they're priced, but Sarah and Jennifer might be interested in carrying them in their store."

Sisters Sarah and Jennifer, both married to Randall cousins, owned and operated Rawhide's popular general store. "They'd have to work out a deal with Monsieur Jalbert," Melissa said. "What I design is his right now."

"Too bad. If you got my name for the Christmas gift exchange, I sure wouldn't mind taking a pair off your hands." She grinned at her cousin.

"Have we drawn names already this year?"

Russ replied, "Yeah. Your mom drew one for you. And I can tell that all the women are going to be hoping you got their name."

"I might make something for a Christmas present. I am already itching to get back to work."

"But could you work here?" Tori asked.

Melissa answered carefully. "I can make a few gifts. But as long as I'm under contract with Monsieur Jalbert, I can't produce any work to sell."

"And when does your contract expire?" she asked.

"January first," Melissa confessed. "But don't mention that to Mom or Dad. They'll think it might mean I could stay here, but—" She cut off that thought. "We'll renew my contract as soon as I return."

Tori was undaunted. She continued to probe. "Why didn't you renew before you came home?"

Melissa looked down at her coffee, avoiding both Russ and Tori's gaze as she said, "There wasn't time. I decided to come home at the last minute."

Before anyone could comment, they were distracted by two men yelling at each other on the other side of the café. Russ, she noticed, kept a particularly watchful eye on them. The argument got heated and the men stood up, going face-to-face. When one of them picked up a knife, Russ wasted no time. He took out his cell phone and dialed 911.

"There's a fight at the café," he said into his phone. "One of the men has a knife,"

"Surely you don't think they're really going to fight?" Melissa asked.

"What, they don't have fights in France?" Russ asked.

Melissa didn't respond.

"Better safe than sorry," he stated. Almost as he spoke, one of the men threw the first punch, and in no time they were knocking chairs over as they fought. The knife fell to the floor, but not before it drew blood from its victim.

As the diners looked on, aghast, the café door opened to admit Harry Gowan.

The badge on his winter coat announced that he was a member of the Sheriff's Office. His actions left no doubt, either. He waded in and stopped the fighting, though he had to take one man to the ground to get him to halt. He called the other man by name and warned him to back off. When he had them both subdued, he called the hospital to alert them that a patient was on the way.

Russ stood. "I'd better help out." He crossed the room, taking a bunch of napkins to press on the wound of the combatant standing. Harry welcomed his assistance, asking him to escort the man to the hospital, just down the street, while he took the other guy, now in cuffs, to jail.

In a couple of minutes, the normal buzz of conversation was restored, as if nothing had happened.

"Well, that was interesting!" Melissa said in amazement.

"Now you see why everyone in town loves Harry," Tori said. "In the old days, the deputy might've drawn a gun, which would endangered everyone here. But he looks for ways to intervene without that."

"He's certainly impressive, but surely sometimes he has to use a gun."

"Yes, I suppose, but not often. First of all, everyone knows he's a crack shot. Mike tests his men every month. Secondly, have you seen Harry's muscles? They're very impressive."

"Actually, I have. He was doing some weight lifting when I got to the station."

Tori's eyebrows rose once again. "But that was in the men's facility, right?"

"I didn't go in," Melissa hastily said. "I just peeked in to see if I could spot him. And I did. He had his shirt off while he lifted weights."

Her cousin smiled. "And was it worth the look?"

"Oh, yes," Melissa said with a sigh. "Unfortunately,

the guys got so perturbed that I opened the door to a 'men's facility,' as they kept calling it, that I had no choice but to close it."

Tori laughed out loud. "Honey, if that story makes its way to your dad, you'll never hear the end of it!"

"He wasn't naked." Instead of saying it in a defensive tone, Melissa wore a small smile, making Tori think she was imagining that very picture.

"It's a good thing," she said. "But I think you've hit on the problem you're having with Harry."

"What do you mean?"

"I think you may have embarrassed him. Harry's a very modest person."

"Tori, it was just his chest. If we went swimming, I'd see that much of him. That can't be it."

"Maybe it's the way you looked at him that disturbed him."

"I don't know what you mean," Melissa said nonchalantly.

"Did you gaze at him as if you were imagining him without the shorts?"

"I did not!" Melissa protested. But her reddening cheeks told a different story.

Tori broke out in laughter. "Maybe you should try for more modesty when you see him at Sunday dinner."

"Are you sure he'll be there?"

"I think so. He may even be there for Thanksgiving and Christmas."

"Oh." It came out more of a moan than a reply.

As if saving her from further embarrassment, their food was delivered just then, along with Russ's pie.

"Will Russ come back for this?" Melissa asked.

"If he doesn't, I'll get it boxed up and take it back to the office."

They ate in silence for several minutes, before Tori asked, "Did Camille mention her health problems to you?"

Melissa's head jerked up. "What are you talking about? Mom's fine."

"Okay." Tori lowered her eyes, staring at her sandwich.

"Don't brush me off after asking that question. What's going on with Mom?"

"You really ought to ask Caroline. But it appears Camille will have to have a complete hysterectomy. Apparently she's asked them to hold off until after you've gone."

"Why does she have to have it? And who will take care of her?"

"I don't know the answers to those questions. Again, you need to ask Caroline."

"Will she tell me? Does Dad know?"

"I'm not sure, Melissa. I'll probably get in trouble for telling you, but I thought you should know."

"Of course I should!" She pushed her plate away. "I'm going to go see Caroline right now." She reached into her purse for her wallet.

Tori stopped her. "No, Melissa, it's my treat. Consider it a welcome-home present. I've missed you."

"Thanks, Tori," Melissa said, standing and bending down to kiss her cousin's cheek. Then she rushed toward the door, anxious to find out about her mother.

In her mind she debated the information Tori had given her. If her condition was serious, wouldn't her mother have told her? Wouldn't she have gone ahead and had the surgery? Why would she wait until after Christmas? It came every year. Surely she would— Maybe that was it. Maybe they'd told her there would be no more Christmases.

Melissa started sobbing as that thought took hold. She'd been away for six years, and she'd missed all that time with her mother. But her mom wasn't old. What was going on?

She wasn't even aware of the tears that streamed from her eyes. Arriving at the hospital, she reached for the door just as someone came out. She pushed past him and was surprised when he caught her arm.

It was Harry Gowan.

"What's wrong? Can I help?"

"No. I have to find Caroline." She tugged on her arm, but Harry didn't let go.

"She's patching up the guy who got cut. You'll have to wait a few minutes. Come in and sit down. I'll tell them you're here to see Caro. Is it— I mean, are you sick?"

"No, but I need to see her at once!"

He led her to the waiting area. "Just sit here. I'll be right back out as soon as I talk to her."

Melissa wondered why he could talk to Caro and she couldn't. Caro was her cousin, not his!

She fixed her gaze on the door through which he had disappeared, trying to be patient, but her thoughts were bouncing off the walls of her mind.

Harry came back out and sat down beside her on the couch. "She's got about ten more minutes of stitching up the guy. Then she'll be out to talk to you. I told her what you said, that you needed to speak to her."

He pulled out a handkerchief and started wiping her cheeks as if she were a child. Leaning closer, he said, "It won't do me any good to mop you up if you keep crying."

Melissa stared at him as if she couldn't comprehend his words.

When he reached out to her again, she tried to pull away, but he held her in place and pressed his handkerchief to her cheeks once more.

One of the nurses opened the door. "Harry?"

He stood. "Come on, Melissa. Caroline's free now."

Melissa followed him, so anxious to see her cousin she didn't even think about why Harry was with her.

Caroline turned as they entered her office. "Melissa, what's wrong?"

"You have to tell me! Mom—"

"Did your mother say anything to you?" Caroline's tone changed from a concerned cousin's to that of a physician.

Melissa shook her head.

"Then I can't discuss her case with you, not without her permission."

Melissa took a deep breath, gathering herself together. "Give me the phone. I'll call her and get permission."

"Melissa, she didn't want to spoil your holidays at home," Caroline said softly.

Melissa ignored her and dialed. As she did, she heard Harry ask Caroline, "Is she going to be okay to drive herself home? She was sobbing as she came in, and the tears haven't stopped."

"I'll make sure she's okay, Harry. Thanks for taking care of her."

"My pleasure. Call me if you need me." He left without a word to her. Before she could call out to him, her mother answered the phone.

Without preamble, Melissa blurted, "Mom, I have to know how you are. I won't let you sacrifice yourself just so I can enjoy the holidays. I want to help take care of you. It's my privilege."

She had to push her mother to get permission to talk with Caroline. And she had to promise not to tell her father. Melissa couldn't believe her mom was keeping something this important a secret from her husband. It was another example of her mother's strength that few people ever saw.

"Thanks, Mom," she said. "Now tell Caroline it's okay." She handed the phone to her cousin.

After speaking to Camille a moment, Caroline hung

up the phone. "I wasn't sure you'd convince her, Melissa, but I'm glad you did."

"Me, too. Now tell me."

"Your mother has a tumor on one of her ovaries. Since she's past childbearing age, we suggested she have a complete hysterectomy."

Melissa studied Caroline's face. "What are you not telling me?"

The woman hesitated, and finally said, "I was hoping to impress you with my doctorly manner so you wouldn't ask questions."

Melissa said nothing, just continuing to stare at her cousin.

With a sigh, Caroline said, "There's the possibility of cancer."

"Then why in hell are you waiting? Won't it improve her chance of survival the sooner it's treated?" Melissa demanded.

"Yes, and we explained that to your mom. We also told her it's possible it's not cancer. But she refused surgery until after you went back to France. She promised we could operate the moment she put you on a plane back to France."

Melissa shook her head. Her worry turned to anger. "I'm going to wring her neck just before I march her down here." Then, realizing what she'd said, she asked, "Can you do the operation here?"

"Yes. Both Jon and I have a lot of experience with

this type of surgery. It's not unusual. And we've expanded the clinic since I came back home."

That was true. Melissa hadn't stopped to notice before how big and up-to-date the facility was, compared to when she'd lived in Rawhide six years ago. Caroline and their cousin-in-law, Jon Wilson, must have worked day and night to elevate the level of care they could provide right here in Rawhide. If anyone was capable of that, she knew Caroline was.

"You've done a hell of a job, Caro," she said.

"Thanks." Caroline smiled. "Jon and I can clear our schedules with a day's notice. I hope you can convince your mother. I had no idea she had such steel inside of her."

"She doesn't reveal it unless an issue is important to her. *I* can't believe she hasn't told Dad."

"You can't tell him, either," Caroline warned. "Not unless she agrees."

Melissa nodded. "I'll talk to Mom now. I'll call you and let you know what she says." She hugged her cousin, grateful for her expertise and support.

As she made her way to the door, Caro called out to her.

"I almost forgot. Harry wanted to know if you would be okay to drive home. It might be nice if you stopped off at his office to tell him you're okay."

Melissa wrinkled her nose. "He'll probably run in the opposite direction."

Caroline gazed at her in surprise. "He seemed very concerned when he brought you in here. Harry is the sweetest man in town, next to Mike, of course." She grinned.

"He didn't look too sweet when he was breaking up the fight in the café."

"Well, no, he knows when he needs to be sweet, like when he found you sobbing. Not when he's breaking up a fight."

Melissa had to admit the logic in Caro's response. And she acquiesced. "Okay, I'll stop by and thank Harry. Then I'm going home to fight Mom."

"I hope you win," Caroline said, her face suddenly serious.

Melissa left the hospital, wrapping her coat more tightly around her. In one pocket she felt a damp cloth, and pulled out a man's handkerchief. It must be Harry's. She had a vague memory of him wiping her cheeks.

She received some curious stares as she walked along the sidewalk in Rawhide, where she'd grown up. It seemed almost no one remembered her, except for her cousins. Thank goodness for them, she thought. It certainly seemed strange to be almost anonymous in a town like Rawhide.

She made a mental note to ask Caro how it felt being away for so long and coming back to town.

Her mother had told her about Caroline's belief that she couldn't have children. She hadn't wanted to come home from Chicago, where she did her internship, because all the Randalls seemed focused on babies. Then she'd met the sheriff and they'd fallen in love and gotten married one Christmas, and now she and Mike Davis had two little boys.

Melissa knew the family thought the world of Mike. But she herself wasn't ready to settle down. Especially in Rawhide. It was like a company town, and the company was named The Randalls. It seemed at least half the population was kin to her.

Deep in her reverie, she almost walked past the Sheriff's Office. Stopping, she opened the door and stepped in. There sat Harry Gowan, doing some paperwork. She cleared her throat.

Without lifting his head, Harry said, "You got anything to report, Wayne?"

Blinking in surprise, she said, "There was an hysterical female, but she's recovered."

He got to his feet and walked around his desk to where Melissa stood. "How are you doing?"

"I'm fine. I wanted to thank you for helping me. I was…a little distressed."

"A little?" he questioned with a smile.

She lifted her chin. "Yes, a little." Then she remembered she needed to keep him in a good mood so he'd agree to her request. "I, uh, need to ask you something."

"Sure. What is it?"

"I know I lost my temper and I'm sorry, but…could you not tell my father about our meeting this morning?"

"You mean about opening the door when you shouldn't have? And shoving the cookies at me and stomping off?"

She gritted her teeth. Did he have to list every offense? "Yes, that's what I mean."

"I think I can manage to forget that." He smiled at her. "The cookies were really good, by the way."

"I'm glad you liked them," she said, but she didn't smile. "I should warn you that my father was match-making. You need to be on your guard."

Harry looked puzzled. "Why would he do that?"

"He wants me to stay here in Rawhide. He's trying to find someone to marry me."

Harry grinned and raised his brows. "That shouldn't be too difficult."

"If that's a compliment, thank you, but I don't think you understand what I'm saying. Dad has chosen *you* as the prime candidate for my not-so-future husband. You'd better start running in the other direction whenever you see me."

"Assuming I'm not interested."

"It doesn't matter if you are or not," she told him, her voice firm. "I'm going back to France after Christmas."

"Oh, yeah? Then I might as well kiss you goodbye," he said, as if his words were normal, acceptable.

Without any more warning than that, he pulled her into his arms and planted a kiss on her lips like none she'd ever received. When he had her reeling, he abruptly put her away from him.

"Have a nice trip, Melissa Randall."

She stared at him blankly, unable to figure out what

she was supposed to do. Then reality poured in and she glared at him. "I will!"

And she left the Sheriff's Office the same way she had earlier.

Chapter Three

Harry buried his head in his arms after Melissa Randall left the office. He figured he'd just made a bad mistake. He'd been tempted by her several times since he'd met her, but he'd merely imagined how it could be between them. Now he knew.

She had the most kissable lips he'd ever tasted. She fit against him perfectly.

Could she be right? Could her father be looking for a husband to keep her at home?

Harry didn't want that role. Forcing a woman to do something she didn't want to do was a losing proposition. He'd seen it in his parents. His mother had had hopes of going to Hollywood and being a star. His father had gotten her pregnant and married her, to keep her with him. They'd had a miserable marriage, and he and his sister had suffered.

He thought he'd learned that lesson, but when he finished college he'd almost made the same mistake as his father. The woman he'd been seriously dating had wanted to go to Denver, a big city, and he'd chosen Rawhide. He'd assumed she'd change her mind and come with him. Fortunately for both of them, she'd gone to Denver.

Forced relationships meant someone was sacrificing something that mattered a lot. He suspected whatever Melissa was doing in France—and he didn't know what that was—it mattered to her a great deal. If she chose to live abroad, then there was no hope for a relationship. He could accept that.

As long as he kept his distance.

"Harry? What's wrong? Are you sick?"

One of the other deputies had entered.

"No, Wayne, I'm fine. I was just thinking."

"Where's the sheriff?"

"He went out to the Miller place, south of town. They think they've been having some cattle rustling out there, and he wanted to look around."

"We haven't had any cattle rustling in a while. Hope we don't have it start up again. Is that what you're worrying about?"

"Uh, yeah. The holidays are a bad time to be hit by rustlers," Harry said, hoping he sounded believable. Compared to the attraction he felt for Melissa Randall, rustling was a small blip on the radar.

The door opened again and Mike Davis, sheriff of their county and husband to Dr. Caroline Randall Davis, came in.

Harry wondered how difficult it had been for Mike,

being attracted to a Randall woman. He'd never really asked him about that.

Before he could do so, Wayne asked about the cattle rustlers. "Did you find anything, Sheriff?"

"Yeah. They were hit pretty hard. It looks like the rustlers pulled up an 18-wheeler, let down a ramp and herded what cattle they could find into the truck, then drove off."

"That's going to make them hard to catch," Harry said.

"Yeah. We need to look at all the ranches along the county road. I'd bet they'll hit again with the same MO."

Harry jumped up and walked to the big map on the wall beside the door to the workout facility. "Besides the Miller ranch, there's the Howser place, the Douglas place, the Windom ranch and the Haney ranch."

"Write those down, Wayne," Mike ordered. "Let's assume the rustlers stick to the south. We need to notify those ranchers to move their cattle away from any pasture alongside the road."

Mike looked at the schedule of deputies on duty. "Wayne, I'm going to leave you in charge. Harry, I'll take the first two and you take the second two. Let's warn them to move their herds before nightfall."

"Yes, sir." Harry wanted to ask to swap the Haney place for either of the others, but he wouldn't do that. The Haney place was Griff Randall's ranch. He and his son, John, ran the ranch Griff had inherited from his father, Bill Haney. Bill had been married when he and the only Randall daughter, Jake's and the others' aunt, had gotten together.

She'd gone to Chicago, pregnant and alone. She'd had Griff and taught him some bitter lessons. When she died, Griff had come back to Rawhide only to bury his mother, prepared to hate the father he'd never known. But he'd found there were two sides to every story, and his mother had lied to him.

Bill Haney had been so grateful to have made peace with his only son, he'd left everything to him. Griff, in turn, had never changed the name of his father's ranch, though he had kept the name Randall himself.

And, of course, that ranch was where Melissa was.

"There isn't a problem, is there, Harry?" Mike asked, breaking into his thoughts.

Harry realized he was still standing there, not having moved after being given his orders.

"No, there's no problem, Mike. I'm on my way."

At least no problem he was willing to talk about.

"I WANT YOU TO HAVE the surgery at once." Melissa started talking as soon as she opened the kitchen door and saw Camille sitting at the table. "It's silly—"

Her mother held up a hand to halt her tirade. "It's my decision, Melissa."

Taking a deep breath, she sat opposite her mother at the table and tried calm reasoning. "I know it is, Mom. But your health is too important to play games with."

"I'd just prefer to wait till after the holidays." She gave Melissa a weak smile. "I've waited six years to have you at the Thanksgiving table with the family."

Melissa reached across and squeezed her hand. "You can still have that, Mom. But the faster you get this problem dealt with, the faster you'll recover. You know," she said seriously, "I want you around to be a grandmother to my children."

"That'll be hard to do if you're living in France."

"It can't happen at all if you're dead," Melissa snapped. At her mother's stricken look, she was immediately sorry for her tone. Before she could apologize, he father's booming voice nearly shook the kitchen.

"What are you talking about?" Griff stood stockstill at the kitchen door.

As much as Melissa ached to tell him, she couldn't. Only her mother could do that. She looked at Camille. "You've got to tell him, Mom."

Camille just turned away, a stubborn look on her face.

"Tell me what? What does she need to tell me, Melissa?" Griff advanced to the table, concern and apprehension etched into his expression.

"Mom," Melissa pleaded.

Finally, Camille looked at her husband. "I need some surgery and I want to wait until after the holidays. That's all."

"What kind of surgery?"

Melissa said nothing, but kept her gaze pinned on her mother's face.

"A—a hysterectomy." Camille turned away again, as if she was ashamed.

Griff sank down in the chair beside his wife. "Why?"

Melissa looked at her dad and nodded encouragingly.

Camille remained turned away. In a whisper, she said, "I have a tumor on my ovary."

"And a hysterectomy will take care of it?"

She nodded.

"Then why are you going to wait?"

"Thanksgiving is coming and Melissa is here and—"

"Nonsense," Griff said, cutting her off. "You're not telling me something." He put his arms around Camille. "Honey, what is it?"

She turned then and buried her face in his shoulder. Griff held her close, giving her time to pull herself together. Then he nudged her. "Come on, honey, tell me everything."

Camille sat up slowly. "There's a possibility I have cancer."

Her words were brisk, businesslike, but Griff stared at her as if she'd just released a bomb. "What? Then you need to have the surgery at once! Isn't that true, Melissa?"

"Caroline said the sooner they do the operation, the more likely Mom can recover."

"But I haven't finished Christmas shopping, and there's Thanksgiving dinner," Camille protested.

"Mom, I—"

Camille speared her with a sharp look. "Don't tell me it's for the grandchildren again, Melissa," she ordered sternly. "I've been waiting for them so long I've just about given up!"

Griff reached out and took her face in his hands,

bringing her attention back to him. "Do it for me, sweetheart. I can't make it without you. I need you healthy and happy for a long time. Remember, you promised to grow old with me." He looked into her eyes. "Do it for me. Have the surgery now."

Camille's eyes filled with tears and she nodded.

Griff hugged her then, tightly, and as he held her, he told Melissa, "Call Caroline right now."

She did as her father asked. As Caroline checked her and Jon's schedules, Melissa kept her eyes on her parents, sitting there at the table in each other's arms. It was as if her mother was drawing strength from her husband's embrace. After all these displays of affection, it still amazed Melissa how much they loved each other. She couldn't help wondering if she'd ever find that kind of love. She'd certainly thought she had, but she hadn't come close.

Caroline came back on the line. "Melissa, we can do the surgery in the morning if your mom is willing. That way we won't have to adjust our schedules, because we have nothing planned for Sunday."

"Really? You don't mind?"

"No, we think it will be better. However, it's started snowing and this is supposed to be a big storm. She should come in now and spend the night. That way we'll have her all prepped for the morning."

"Okay. That's what we'll do. Thanks, Caro."

She got off the phone and told her parents what her cousin had said.

Her mother looked petrified. "Now? But I was going to try to get more done before—"

Griff cut her off. "That's great, Melissa. I'm going in with your mother and I'll spend the night there with her."

"I'll go, too."

"No, child, your mother and I will be together. You come in the morning for the surgery. Okay?"

Melissa leaned forward and kissed his cheek. "Okay, Dad." She knew her father had been hard hit by the news and wanted time with his wife. "But you promise to take good care of her."

"You know I will. Now, go help her pack a bag, please."

"Why is it that I have no say in what's happening to me?" Camille complained.

"Because you never put yourself first, my love. But this time you have to." He kissed her before he said, "I'm going to go talk to John before we leave."

When he went outside, Griff saw someone parked near the barn. He hurried out of the chilly wind to find the owner of the truck inside, talking to his son.

"Harry! It's good to see you. Why didn't you come up to the house?"

"Hi, Griff. Good to see you, too. I had some information that I figured you'd need as soon as possible. At this time of the day, I thought you'd be out here."

"What kind of information?"

Harry told him about the cattle rustlers and the need to move the herd.

John spoke up. "I was just coming in to tell you, Dad. We don't have much time before dark."

Griff stood there, staring at them. "I can't help you, Son."

"What are you talking about, Dad? Even if we could afford the loss, we don't want to let these guys get away with rustling, do we?"

"No, Son, but your mother is going for surgery as soon as I can get her to the hospital. I just found out about it. She was planning on delaying the operation until Melissa went back to France, but it can't wait."

"Is she all right?" John asked, fear in his voice.

"She will be, but the surgery has to be done at once," Griff said.

"I'll stay and help you, John, if you've got a horse for me," Harry said.

"You don't have to do that," he protested in a slightly embarrassed tone.

"Son, learn to take help when it's offered." Griff turned to Harry. "Thanks. We appreciate it."

"What about Melissa? Is she going with you?" John asked.

"No, she's coming in in the morning. You can come, too, if you want."

"Yeah, I will. But ask Melissa if she can help us now."

Harry stared at John as if he were crazy. But Griff just nodded. "Saddle a horse for her. I'll send her right out."

After Griff walked out of the barn, Harry turned to his friend. "Your sister will help us move the herd?

Do you think she can? I mean, she probably hasn't ridden in years."

"Naw, she doesn't spend all her time making jewelry."

"She makes jewelry?"

"Yeah. You didn't know?"

"Hell, I didn't even know you had a sister, John!" Harry said in exasperation.

John grinned. "I guess I don't talk enough. You want to borrow some chaps?"

"Yeah, if you've got a spare pair. They'll help keep the cold out."

"Sure, here you go," John said, taking down a pair from the Peg-Board on the wall. "You don't have to warn anyone else?"

"Nope. You're the last on the list. We split the ranches up, Mike and I. I need to call him and let him know where I am, though."

"That's fine. You need a phone?"

"No, I'll use my cell." He called the sheriff and told him he was going to help John move his herd, and would be in later. Mike agreed to keep an eye on everything, since Harry had the late shift.

Just as he turned off the phone, the barn door opened and Melissa came in. Her eyes, he noticed, were suspiciously red.

"You all right, sis?" John asked at once.

After a quick look at her brother, Melissa said, "Yes, of course. Mom and Dad are getting in the car if you want to go tell her goodbye."

"Yeah, I'll go do that. I haven't got your horse saddled yet, but I'll do it when I get back."

Harry watched John leave the barn. Then he said abruptly, "Which horse is yours?"

"Maybelle here. She's eight years old, so she can still go."

Harry moved over to check out at the gray mare. "Yeah, she looks good. Are you sure you can stay on?"

"Excuse me? You're talking to a Randall, I'll have you know."

"Yeah, but you're a Randall with a French accent," Harry said with a wry grin. "Which saddle is yours?"

"This one," she said, pointing to one hanging nearby. "But I can saddle her myself."

"No need. Save your energy." He grabbed her saddle and went to work on Maybelle. "John said he has his biggest herd over in the pasture by the county road. And we don't have a lot of time."

"Do *you* know how to ride?" Melissa asked, a smile on her lips.

Harry stopped saddling the horse and looked at her. A man in Rawhide who didn't know how to ride? What did she think he was?

"Of course I know how to ride. And drive cattle." He tilted his hat and gave her a sharp stare. "I would venture a guess I've had more experience at it than you have."

She put her hands on her hips and took a step forward. "You think so, cowboy? Remember, I grew up here."

Harry gave her an assessing look. She'd lost her

drawl and her hair was so short and spiky; even her jeans were designer. Sometimes, he had to admit, it was hard to remember she was from Wyoming. Aside from her little temper tantrums, she seemed sophisticated and...worldly. Anyone could see she'd spent a considerable amount of time outside of Rawhide.

He laughed to himself. Actually, he couldn't wait to see Little Miss Parisian out there riding herd.

He tugged on Maybelle's saddle, found it tight, and stepped back, waving his hand with a flourish. "Your mount awaits, m'lady." Then he cracked a smile and added, "We'll just see who's the rider here."

Melissa took the dare. She speared him with a look and said, "You're on."

Grabbing Maybelle's reins, she led the mare out of the barn, leaving Harry to follow.

Not that it was a bad view, he admitted. He was developing quite a liking for those tight, designer jeans.

John met up with them outside the barn, having said goodbye to his mother. "We're ready," Harry told him.

John nodded resolutely, concern for his mother temporarily replaced by determination to get the job done. He glanced over at his sister. "Get a pair of chaps. It's going to be cold out there. You have good gloves?"

Melissa smiled. "Yes, John," she said patiently. "You know I've done this before."

Harry snickered, but she ignored him. Instead she pointed to a pile of scarves she'd left inside the barn door. "Dad gave me those. Said we'd need them for the cold." She looked at Harry then. "If you wrap one around your face and tie it in back, it'll serve as a kerchief, and keep you warm, too."

Biting back a comment, he put one on, then reached out and tied Melissa's behind her short hair. He expected a complaint but got none. Nor did he get a thank-you.

She pulled a hat on her head, climbing into the saddle and headed out.

John rode alongside Harry into the cold, windy pasture. Had it been any other day of the week, They'd have had a number of cowboys to help out. But it was Saturday, and all the men had already gone into town. Probably all lined up for a beer already, Harry figured. Just like last night, when he'd first seen Melissa.

That scene had replayed in his head a few times—how beautiful she'd looked sitting there, sipping her beer. He wondered how different things would have turned out if he'd taken her up on her request for a dance.

He'd never know.

Once they reached the pasture by the county road, there was no time for thinking. There was a herd to gather.

Snow had begun to fall and the temperature was dropping sharply. John kept looking up at the sky, but Harry didn't bother. Mike had already alerted them to the forecast, and it was not good. They were in for a substantial snowfall, on top of what was already on the ground.

Luckily, the herd was mostly Herefords. Their red coats showed up better in the swirling snow.

They rounded up the large herd, each working hard

at the job. Even Melissa. She rode with skill and knew her way around the herd, Harry would give her that. As much as it pained him to admit it, she held her own.

By the time they dragged themselves back to the barn, it was after eight o'clock and the three of them were exhausted. The buffeting of the wind was enough to wear anyone out.

Melissa hopped down off of her mare. "If you'll unsaddle Maybelle and give her some oats," she told he men, "I'll get up to the house and start supper for us."

Harry could only stare at her. The words came out of his mouth before he could censor them. "You ride herd and cook, too? Man, you're a rancher's dream!"

As she strode by him, she tipped her nose in the air. "I'm not so sure that a rancher would be my dream, though."

Chapter Four

"I'm not sure my sister's dreams are like those of other women in Rawhide."

John's words reached Harry through his haze. He'd been too intent watching Melissa sashay up to the house to pay his friend any mind. Now he turned to John.

"They wouldn't be, though, would they? I mean, she's been living in Paris for six years." He grinned. "Heck, she's probably the only person in Rawhide who's ever been."

"Not so," John said unsaddling Maybelle. "Mom and Dad went to see her awhile back."

"Did they like it?"

"Mom enjoyed it, but she said she was glad to get back home. Dad didn't have anything good to say about it. He's never been happy that Melissa is living there."

"Yeah, I can imagine. Melissa says he's trying to marry her off to someone here in Rawhide so she'll stay here." Harry didn't look at his friend. He just kept taking care of the horse he'd borrowed.

"I wonder who he's got in mind," John said. When Harry said nothing, John stopped what he was doing and looked at him. "Harry? Do you know who Dad's thinking of?"

"I don't know what your dad is thinking, but Melissa said it's me."

"Really?" John asked eagerly. "That'd be great, Harry! Hey, snap her up at once!"

"That's not how it works, John. Melissa has to be interested. More than interested, she has to want to marry and stay here rather than go back to France. And I don't see that happening. Do you?"

John stood there, looking at him. Finally, he shook his head. "No, I don't see that happening."

"Then you should encourage your dad not to press her on that front. If she married because of him, the marriage wouldn't last. You know how that goes."

"You sound like a voice of experience. You've seen a marriage like that?"

Harry hefted off the saddle and put it in the tack room. "Yeah, my parents'. When they finally divorced it was a relief for all of us."

"I'm sorry, Harry. I didn't know."

"It's not something you go around bragging about. But I think both my parents are happier now. Anyway, that's why I'm not interested in Melissa. She's beautiful and obviously talented, but I don't want an unhappy wife."

He couldn't believe he was using the words *Melissa*

and *wife* in the same thought. He laughed to himself as he absently brushed down the borrowed horse. The matchmaking Randalls were legendary in these parts. But they'd met their match in Melissa.

Once he and John fed the horses, they bundled up again for the trek to the house. The snow was falling heavily now, and blowing around, nearly obliterating the building in front of them. Trudging through the storm they reached the mudroom and shed their coats and boots, which were wet and covered in crusty snow.

Melissa called out from the kitchen. "Come on in. It's almost ready."

Suddenly, Harry hesitated. The scene was almost too domestic. Him coming in from work, Melissa having dinner ready. "Maybe I should go on back to town. I'm supposed to be on duty tonight."

John stared at him. "You've got to be kidding! Didn't you see how bad this storm is? I don't think you're going back to town until it stops, Harry. You'd be crazy to try."

"Well, I'm certainly not spending the night here!"

John ignored him and ushered him inside. "Come in and call Mike. He'll tell you the same thing."

Harry pulled his cell phone off his belt, but found he had no service, probably due to the storm. Now he had to go in and use the house phone.

John led the way into the kitchen.

"Where are you going?" Melissa asked as the men walked through the room.

"To the phone," her brother told her. "Harry wants to drive back to town now."

She looked at Harry. "Are you nuts? It's not safe."

"I'm on duty tonight," he said, as if that was sufficient reason to try.

She raised her chin and gave him a glare as cold as the great outdoors. "And we certainly know how you take your duty seriously."

John looked at him, puzzled. "What does she mean?"

Harry ignored his friend, his eyes never leaving Melissa. So she'd thought about that night at the steak house and bar, too?

Not that it mattered, he reminded himself quickly. Nothing could ever happen between them.

He went to the phone and called Mike, who, as he'd suspected, told him to stay put. The roads were a mess and the day shift deputies were pulling double duty.

"What did Mike say?" John asked as he came to the table.

Harry frowned. "I guess I'm staying, if y'all don't mind putting me up."

Melissa answered before her brother could. "Of course we don't. It'd be pretty rude of us to refuse when you helped move the herd." She put bowls of hot soup in front of them.

"What's this?" John asked.

"French onion soup."

He frowned. "You made us French food? Dad said he almost starved to death before he got home."

"Oh, just try it, John," Melissa said, losing her patience. "It's hardly French. It's onion soup with melted cheese." She muttered, "If you want French, try eating snails."

John looked about ready to pass on dinner.

Harry tried the soup. "Hey, this is good. Did you make it?" he asked Melissa.

"Yes. And thank you." She gave him a smile.

The smile warmed him as much as the hot soup.

They ate silently until the phone rang, shattering the quiet.

John jumped up to answer it. "Hello? Oh, hi, Dad. How's Mom?"

Immediately, Melissa's attention was focused on her brother. Harry watched her, seeing the anxiety she was feeling. It must've been hard to come out with them instead of going to the hospital with her mom.

When Melissa realized he was staring at her, she stiffened and turned to eat the rest of her soup.

"You should've gone with your mom instead of helping us," Harry said softly.

"I wanted to, but Dad needed to be alone with her tonight. He didn't have time to prepare for any separation or the threat of a serious illness."

"They're that close?"

Melissa looked at him in surprise. "Yes. Aren't your parents?"

He gave her a wry look. "Not for a long time. They divorced ten years ago."

"Oh, I'm sorry. I didn't know."

"It's okay. It's not a sensitive subject for me. They're much happier since they split up."

"Are you an only child?"

"No, I have a younger sister. She had a harder time with the divorce. She was just fourteen. She's married now and I don't see her that often. I don't much like her husband."

"How old were you when your folks divorced?"

"Eighteen. That makes me twenty-eight now."

Melissa flashed an embarrassed smile. "I guess I wasn't subtle enough."

"So how old are you?"

"Twenty-six."

"You moved to France when you were twenty? Was your dad crazy?"

Her spine stiffened. "He wasn't crazy at all. He and Mom realized what a great experience it would be for me."

John, who had just hung up the phone, entered the conversation, "You mean, Mom decided it would be a great experience for you, and forced Dad into agreeing."

"How did she do that?" Harry asked.

John rolled his eyes, but Melissa said, "She stopped speaking to him until he gave in."

Harry looked at John, "How long did that take?"

"A couple of days," Melissa stated. Suddenly she noticed John smiling and Harry looking at him, nodding.

"What?"

Her brother shrugged. "I didn't say anything."

She turned to stare at Harry. "Why were you nodding?"

"I was just acknowledging what you said," he replied. He certainly didn't want to tell Melissa that her mother might have withheld more than her conversation. Sleeping on a lonely sofa could convince a man quickly.

"Is this soup all we're having, sis?" John interjected. Harry recognized the subject change.

"Oh! I forgot the steak." Melissa jumped up and headed into the kitchen.

"Good save," Harry whispered.

"I see you thought what I thought. I didn't ask Dad, but I figured if she wasn't speaking to him, even Dad wasn't going to try anything."

Harry laughed.

When John went to help with the steak, declining Harry's offer of assistance, Harry thought about the conversation. Clearly, Melissa's parents had a good marriage. They still loved each other and their children. He wondered how a marriage like that would feel. And if he'd ever find out.

"Here we go," Melissa announced, setting a thick steak down in front of Harry, steam rising from it.

John had followed her to the table, carrying his own plate.

"This looks great. Thanks. I'm just afraid I'll fall asleep before I can finish. Have you noticed that when you warm up after being out in the cold it makes you sleepy?"

"Yes," Melissa said with a chuckle. "Mom used to let us play outside in winter just before lunch. Then she'd feed us and put us to bed at once. We never even complained about naps."

"Sometimes I wish I was still that young," John said with a sigh.

Melissa frowned. "Why, John? Is something wrong?"

"No, not really. It's just…Dad wants me to take over running the ranch, but I can feel him staring over my shoulder all the time."

"Have you told him how you feel?"

Harry cleared his throat. "That would be a little difficult, Melissa."

"Why?" she asked, turning to gaze at him.

Harry sought for words. "It would be like you taking over the cooking. Even if your mother ate what you fixed, you probably would think she was criticizing your cooking in her head."

"No, I wouldn't think that."

Harry looked at John. "I tried."

"Thanks," John said, before he turned to his sister. "It's a macho thing, sis."

"Oh, well, I think that's silly. Dad wouldn't turn it over to you if he didn't believe in your ability."

"Maybe you're right. Maybe it's me having doubts, not Dad."

"I can only tell you your dad always brags about your ranching knowledge when he's talking with the other Randalls," Harry said to reassure his friend.

"See?" Melissa echoed. "Just assume you know the best way to do things."

"And if I'm wrong?"

"It's just possible your father made some mistakes in his time, too," Harry pointed out.

"If Granddad were alive, he could probably tell you," Melissa added.

"You've got to be kidding, Melissa. You know he thought Dad could do no wrong."

"He didn't think you could, either!" Melissa said with a grin.

"Oh, yeah, I'd forgotten that."

"That's a nice memory," Harry said with a smile.

"Didn't you have a grandfather who believed in you?" Melissa asked.

"Nope." He took a bite of his steak and chewed, showing no inclination to add to his statement.

"Did you not have a grandfather?" Melissa asked, leaning toward him, sympathy on her face.

"I had two of them," Harry said. "They were pretty ornery and we didn't see them often. Don't start feeling sorry for me, Melissa. I'm just fine."

Harry may have told her not to feel sorry for him, but Melissa couldn't help it.

She'd tossed and turned for the last hour since coming to bed, but she couldn't shake the thoughts of Harry that had taken hold in her mind.

Not only had his grandfathers been difficult, but his

parents had divorced, and now he had little contact with his only sibling. Poor man.

Everyone thought Harry Gowan was wonderful. Her cousins certainly did. And her father. He wanted her to marry him!

Not that she was even considering such a crazy thing. But her mother's surgery did make her stop and think for the first time. Her entire family was here in Rawhide, and she'd spent the last six years in Europe. Six years that she'd missed being a part of her mother's life.

Not that she didn't have a life of her own to lead in Paris. She had friends and, until a week ago, she'd had Pierre.

But what else?

Your work, said a voice inside her head. But as much as she enjoyed jewelry designing, she wasn't so enamored of Monsieur Jalbert. For the past six months she'd been having doubts about remaining with him, whether she'd actually agree to the contract up for renewal. Or maybe strike out on her own.

Were they dreams? she asked herself. Or pipe dreams?

A master jeweler and shrewd business man, Monsieur Jalbert wielded a lot of power, not only in Paris, but throughout western Europe. With one decree he could make it difficult for her to sell her designs, even downright impossible.

Could she come back to America?

There were certainly cosmopolitan locales that could

rival Paris—New York, San Francisco, maybe. And she'd certainly be closer to her parents.

In her line of work, she could set up shop anywhere in a major city where she could market her jewelery.

Wait a minute! said that inner voice. She was going back to Paris. She had the return ticket to prove it!

Outside her window, the wind knocked bare tree branches against the house. Earlier she'd found their rhythmic tapping somewhat soothing, but now the noise made her anxious.

She needed a drink to settle herself down. Back in Paris she usually had wine with dinner, or sherry afterward with some friends. She found it helped her sleep, especially when she was jittery or stressed.

She doubted her parents had any on hand. Then she remembered the bottle of French wine she'd brought them from the vineyard in Bordeaux she'd visited a couple months ago.

It had been a wonderful afternoon, strolling through the winery, sampling different wines until she found the one she liked best. Too bad the memory included Pierre. It was supposed to have been a romantic getaway weekend; it turned out to be nothing of the kind.

Banishing the recollection, she grabbed her robe and went in search of the wine. Her parents wouldn't mind if she opened the bottle.

The orange embers in the living room fireplace were keeping the house warm, and she didn't bother putting on the robe, instead throwing it over a chair on the way to the kitchen. In no time she found the bottle and poured herself a glass, which she took back into the living room.

The big club chair was as comfortable as she remembered. Facing the fireplace, it was her favorite place to sit. She would put her feet up and let the fire warm them, while gazing into the flames. Melissa had spent many a winter afternoon in this chair with a pad on her lap while she worked on her designs.

"You're the picture of contentment."

The male voice startled her. She jumped, nearly spilling her wine, and turned toward the sound.

There, sprawled out on the big sofa, was Harry Gowan. He was wrapped in her mother's handmade floral quilt, his head sticking out one end, his feet the other.

"What are you doing here?" she demanded.

"You invited me, remember?"

Yes, she did. She'd just figured John had put him up in one of the spare rooms after she'd gone to bed. She told Harry so.

"No need to go to so much trouble. The couch was fine." He smiled, "At least until you woke me."

"Sorry. I—I couldn't sleep."

"Worried about your mother?" he asked. As he sat up, the quilt fell to his lap, revealing his bare chest. In the glowing firelight it looked bronzed, each muscle rippling as he breathed in and out.

She couldn't take her eyes off him. His brown hair

was sleep-tousled, his jaw shadowed by a hint of stubble. She wondered what he wore underneath that quilt; no clothing was visible.

"She'll be fine. Caro's a great doctor. There's no need to worry."

"She's my cousin, Harry. I know what kind of doctor she is."

"You *have* been away for a while. I'm not sure you know how well equipped the hospital is. Though it's probably not what you're used to." He eyed the glass she was holding. "Are you drinking wine?"

"Do you have a problem with that?" she asked.

He shook his head. "Not my personal favorite."

"Back in Paris everyone drinks it, even children."

He gave her a crooked smile as he looked around the cozy room. "In case you haven't noticed, Melissa, you're not in Paris anymore."

He hadn't spoken truer words.

But in Paris she didn't have a matchmaking father breathing down her neck, determined to marry her off to the local deputy. No matter how handsome he was.

She pulled the collar of her nightgown closed and stood up. "I've got to get some sleep. Good night, Mr. Gowan."

Before he could reply, she strode out of the room, forgetting her robe until she got back to bed. Damned if she'd return for it.

There was something about Harry that made her react, like a spark to tinder. Given that incendiary quality, she'd best keep her distance.

She got into bed, once more tossing and turning in her quest for sleep. But she couldn't relax. And she knew the reason why.

He was on the couch in the living room.

IT WAS STILL DARK when John woke Harry. He roused him from a deep sleep on the sofa.

"Sorry, buddy, but the storm has stopped and Melissa and I are going to try to make it to the hospital before they start the surgery. You can sleep longer if you want. Just leave whenever you like."

Harry sat up and his eyes lit on the blue robe across the back of the chair nearest the kitchen. So he hadn't dreamed it; Melissa had been here.

He hoped John didn't see the robe and start asking questions.

"I'll follow you into town, John. That way, if either of us has any trouble, we have help."

"That'd be great. Hey, you want breakfast?"

Harry looked into the lighted kitchen but saw no sign of Melissa. "No, I'll catch it at the café."

He didn't see her until they left the house. She was already in the truck waiting for John when the men came outside. She looked tense and apprehensive, and Harry knew she hadn't slept a wink all night.

They started toward town, ahead of the snowplow. All told, it looked as if a foot and a half of snow had fallen overnight and about half of that remained on the roadway, having iced in the predawn freeze.

The twenty-minute drive took almost an hour. When they reached town, Harry followed them to the hospital. He figured he'd wait and see if everything was okay. After they began the surgery, he could take Melissa and John to the café and buy them breakfast.

They found Griff sitting in the waiting room alone. Melissa ran forward and hugged him. "Are we too late? Have they started already?"

"Yeah, about five minutes ago, but Camille was kind of loopy before that."

"How long will the surgery take?" Harry asked.

"About three hours," Griff said, automatically checking his watch.

"Then why don't you come to the café with me, and I'll buy you all breakfast? I owe you for the meal I had last night."

"No, I can't." Griff tucked his hands in his pockets and began pacing the waiting room.

John and Harry looked at each other.

Melissa said, "I'll stay here with Dad and you two go get breakfast."

"No, I'll stay," John said. "I can talk to him about cows. That'll settle his mind. If you talk to him about Paris, he may lose control completely."

Melissa opened her mouth to protest, but Harry cut her off.

"Come on, Melissa. We'll bring them back some breakfast," he said, hoping she would accept his invitation.

"Okay." She went over and hugged her dad again, whispering something to him that the other two couldn't hear. Then she headed for the door. "Are you coming, Harry?"

"Right behind you, Melissa," he said, and waved goodbye to John.

The café had just opened and wasn't busy yet. Harry ordered eggs and bacon, with hot biscuits. Melissa ordered French toast.

"Did you order that just because it has 'French' in its name?" he asked with a grin.

"No. I ordered it because it was always my favorite when I was a little girl." She stared across the empty café as if she were seeing into the past. It was the same look she'd worn last night by the fire, he noted, remembering the blue nightgown that matched her eyes. "I had a great childhood."

"I guess you did. You have great parents."

"Yes, I know. And don't tell me I shouldn't have gone away," she declared. "I had to!"

"I'm sure they understand."

"I don't know."

"I think that's one of the toughest things about being a parent," Harry said. "One day you're protecting and nurturing your child, and the next, the kid insists he's all grown up, and moves out. That must leave a terrible hole in the family."

"You're going to make me start crying, Harry, and I don't want to do that here."

"I didn't mean to. I'm sorry. I just never thought like a parent before, never thought about what it must be like to have kids, until now." Suddenly self-conscious, he looked down at the tabletop. He gave a nervous laugh. "They'd better bring our food real soon before I make a total fool of myself."

Melissa gave a watery chuckle. "Perfect timing. Here comes our breakfast."

The waitress delivered their breakfast with a friendly smile and then headed back into the kitchen. Harry took a drink of his coffee. "I was missing my caffeine. I should never talk in the morning before I have my coffee."

"I'm the same way," she said, having regained control of her emotions. "I should've made a pot before we left home."

"As it was we didn't get here in time. We'll take some back to your father and brother."

"I think they have coffee at the hospital."

"Yeah, but it won't be as good. I've got a thermos at the Sheriff's Office. I'll go get it after we eat, and have them fill it up."

"That would be great, Harry."

He looked at her plate. "You know, that French toast looks pretty good. I may have to try it one day."

"Here, I'll give you a bite."

Harry leaned forward and let her put a forkful, covered with syrup, into his mouth. "Man, I had no idea what I've been missing. That's like having dessert for breakfast!"

"No more than pancakes. It has egg on the bread, so it's kind of healthy," she assured him with a smile.

"I think if I listen to you, I'll end up liking everything French." *Including you.* He was grateful he didn't voice that last part.

"Even the escargot?" she teased.

He shook his head and made a face. "Never. That's why they use that fancy name. Nobody'd ever eat it if they knew they were snails."

Laughing, Melissa sat back in her seat. "You know, Harry, I didn't think I could possibly enjoy breakfast this morning, but you're making it fun. Thank you."

"My pleasure. Especially since all I'm doing is talking to a beautiful woman."

He was starting to regret his frank statement, but then Melissa smiled. "Everyone is right about you, Harry. You are sweet. Too bad I'm going back to Paris."

Why did she think something could develop between them? There wasn't a chance. He thought the world of Griff Randall, but the man had chosen the wrong bachelor to hitch up with his daughter. "Yeah, 'cause I sure fit in with the Randalls," he said sarcastically.

"Why don't you?"

He was about to go into all the reasons, the main two being his lack of family and funds. The Randalls were among the richest people in the state. How would he fit in on a deputy's salary?

He quickly changed the subject. "We'd better place the orders for your dad and John."

"Already?"

"Yeah, hurry up and eat. I'll go order their food."

He got up and left the table. Getting away from Melissa was essential for his well-being.

When he placed the order, he told the waitress he would go get a thermos for coffee to take to the hospital.

"Don't bother. We've got one here we can loan you," she replied. "It's the least we can do after you cleaned up that fight yesterday."

"I'll take you up on that offer, but you don't owe me anything. I was doing my job. Just holler when the order is ready."

He went back to the table to finish his breakfast.

"Are they going to let us know when it's ready?"

Melissa, he noticed, never touched her French toast again.

"Yeah. Have you finished?" he asked.

"I'm not as hungry as I thought," she said, her eyes filled with worry.

"Melissa, you need to eat breakfast so you can help your mother later. She'll need you to be strong for her."

"I hadn't thought of that." She picked up her fork. "Of course I can eat some more."

Harry watched her hurry through her meal, amazed at the love she had for her mother. And her father and brother. Everyone in the family loved each other. How had she managed to stay away for six years?

It was a question he couldn't ask.

They took the food back to the hospital and sat with Griff and John as they ate. They all had to urge Griff to eat his breakfast, using Harry's reasoning—that he had to be strong for Camille.

They were still drinking coffee when Jon and Caroline came to the door in their scrubs.

Chapter Five

Harry figured it was a good thing Griff had set his coffee cup down on the lamp table before they appeared, because the rancher jumped up and crossed the room, unaware of anything but the outcome of the surgery.

"How is Camille?" he demanded.

"She's fine, Uncle Griff," Caroline said, smiling.

Jon added, "We didn't see any sign of cancer. We're going to go ahead and send tissue to the lab to be sure, but we think the prognosis is excellent."

Harry and John rushed to Griff's sides to shore him up as relief ran through him. "Thank God, thank God," the older man muttered. "Thanks to both of you."

Melissa, who had joined them, looked at Caroline. "When can we see her?"

"She's still in recovery. It will be a little while yet before she comes to. A nurse will come out and get you, one at a time, to go see her. Then we'll move her to her room."

John asked, "How long will she have to stay?"

"Just a couple of days. As long as there is someone at home to keep an eye on her...." Jon said, looking at Melissa.

"Yes, I'll be there."

"Good. Well, we're going to get cleaned up and check on her again before we go home to our families."

They all thanked the doctors again and sat back down. Griff buried his face in his hands.

"Are you all right, Dad?" Melissa asked.

"Yeah. I'm just so relieved. I couldn't face losing Camille."

"Neither could we," John said.

"No," Melissa said. "I've missed six years of her life. I'd never forgive myself if— But now she'll be fine. I'll make sure of that."

"Does that mean you're planning on staying?" Griff asked.

"No, Dad, but I'll come back more often."

He abruptly got up and began pacing back and forth again.

John glared at his sister.

Melissa turned away, tears in her eyes.

Harry wanted to reach out to her, to help her, but he actually agreed with Griff and John. Couldn't she see how important it was to all of them that she come home?

Not that it was any of his business. Of course not. She might be the most kissable woman he'd ever met, but he knew better than to lose his heart to someone who didn't want to live in Rawhide. This was his home and he wasn't leaving.

John stood as his father moved past. "You might as well sit down, Dad. You've got to think of Mom. She's going to need you to be strong for her."

Griff looked at him as if he hadn't heard his words.

Melissa added her plea. "Mom will be leaning on you, Dad."

"And what about you?" Griff roared. "She'll need you, too!"

"And I'm going to be there for her, Dad. You know I will." Melissa sat back down. "I'll take care of her."

"And then you'll leave again!"

"Dad," John interrupted. "Now's not the time to fight this battle."

"You're right," Griff said with a sigh as he sank into his chair. "But we will fight it, Melissa. I've been too tolerant of your staying in France."

"I'm an adult, Dad, not a child," Melissa said indignantly.

Harry stood. "I think it's time you and I go find some lunch for everyone, Melissa. You all need to eat to keep up your strength. Come on."

She resisted momentarily, then picked up her coat and started to join Harry. Suddenly she stopped. "Dad, I don't have any money to buy lunch. Harry paid for breakfast and—"

"Sorry, Harry, I didn't think," Griff immediately said. He pulled out his billfold and offered a fifty dollar bill.

"No, Griff, it's all right. I'll —"

"I insist you take this. You've taken care of all of us this morning and you're not even family. The least I can do is pay for lunch."

Melissa reached out and took the money. "I'll bring you back your change, Dad."

Harry grabbed Melissa's arm and dragged her to the door. "Put on your coat."

"Yes, boss, I will." She shrugged into the warm garment. He'd already put his on. As soon as she was wrapped up, she followed him out into the snowy weather.

"Isn't it a little early for lunch?" Melissa asked, suddenly realizing it was only ten o'clock.

"Yeah, but you weren't helping the situation in there. I thought you needed an exit. We can walk around town, get you some fresh air and exercise. I don't think you get that much in France."

"Oh, really? You think you know so much about life in France? For your information we walk everywhere. People usually don't own cars in Paris. They have good public transportation and walk a lot!"

"And you think life there is that much better than life here in Wyoming?"

"Yes! If you want to eat out, you have a million different places to go. Here you have only one or two."

"Don't you believe in home cooking? Do you eat out all the time?"

"It's convenient. I work hard all day long. I don't want to work hard at dinnertime, too."

"You work regular hours?" he asked in surprise.

"No. I work a lot longer than most people. I kind of work the hours a rancher does. Daylight hours."

"You don't work with lighting?"

"Yes, I do, but I don't prefer it. My place was built by an artist and allows in a lot of natural light."

"So you're definitely going back?"

She didn't look at him, but said, "Yes, I am."

"Damn. Then I guess I'd better kiss you goodbye again." Pulling her into the shadows of a doorway, he wrapped his arms around her and bent to kiss those lips that were driving him crazy.

She didn't resist. In fact, she slipped her arms around his neck and willingly participated in the kiss. Which made it all the more addictive for Harry.

How long they would've continued, he didn't know. But they were interrupted by one of his fellow deputies.

"Hey, you two should find a warmer— Oh, Harry! Uh, I didn't realize— Maybe you should go indoors."

"Yeah, Wayne, thanks." His face red, Harry took Melissa by the arm and started walking again. As they went, he bent down to say, "You'd better leave soon, or I'm going to be fired for assaulting you on the street!"

"It wasn't an assault!" Melissa retorted indignantly. "It was a goodbye kiss. That's different."

"Yeah, except that you're not leaving today."

"He didn't know that."

"If he didn't, he will tomorrow," Harry muttered.

They walked in silence after that, except for the greetings Harry exchanged with townspeople who passed.

Finally, she asked, "Do you know everyone in town?"

"I reckon. Why?"

"I don't know a lot of them. Those I do know don't even recognize me. I feel like a stranger, and I was born here!"

"That's what happens when you leave for another continent and don't come home."

"I think it's because I cut my hair and spiked it."

"Why did you do that?"

"Because it's all the rage in Paris."

"Well, it's not in Rawhide," he drawled, still moving.

"How long are we going to walk?"

"I don't know. We've got awhile before it's really lunchtime. I figure your dad will get some rest if he's not fighting with you. Your mom will wake up and he'll go in and see her. He'll be a lot calmer when we get back."

"But I want to see Mom, too."

"She's not going anywhere, honey. But your dad will go in first, even if you're there."

"I know. I'm just worried about her," Melissa said, lowering her head.

Harry put his arm around her, and she leaned into him, drawing on his strength.

"Maybe you'll even get to feed her her lunch when we get back."

"Do you think they'll let her eat lunch?"

"Why not, if she's awake and feeling good? And if you feed her it'll free up a nurse to do other things."

"Then let's go get our lunches so I'll be finished and can feed her."

"We're getting there," he assured her. They'd walked all the way to the end of town. He turned her around and they started back to the center where the café was located.

"What should we get them? Is Thursday still enchilada day?"

"Of course. Things don't change around here that much. Since it's Sunday, we can get hamburgers or maybe some pot roast."

"So tell me what there is to see and do in Paris," Harry asked, surprising Melissa.

"Do you think you're going to visit someday?"

"You never know. When you were living in Rawhide, did you expect to go to France?"

"No, not until I started taking French in college."

"So tell me about Paris."

"There's a million things to see and do. The museums are incredible. Not just the Louvre, where the *Mona Lisa* hangs. The Centre Pompidou features modern art. The building itself is a work of art. And there's an impressionist museum across the Seine, on the Left Bank."

"Isn't there anything other than museums?"

"Of course. There's the Père Lachaise burial ground, where Jim Morrison is buried, and—"

"You go visit a cemetery? Isn't that a little bizarre?"

"No, some famous people are buried there. And there

are lots of street performers to see, and outdoor cafés where you can sit and watch the people go by. The river and its bridges are wonderful, too."

"You got me there. We don't have a river in the middle of Rawhide."

"And the churches are spectacular. Notre Dame, of course, but there are others. And then there's the Eiffel Tower."

"Have you been up it?"

She nodded. "Everyone goes. It gives you the best view of the city. That and over in Montmartre you can ride a cable car to the top of the hill, where the Sacre Coeur Cathedral looks down on the city."

"Okay, you've convinced me that Paris is an exciting place to visit. But don't you get tired of it after a while?" Harry asked.

"Do you get tired of living in Rawhide?" she asked, taking him by surprise.

"Of course not. It's always changing." He sat back and stared at her. "Okay, you've made your point."

"It's strange, isn't it? I was born here and went away. You were born somewhere else and came here."

"Are you saying you'll never move back here?"

"I don't know about the future. Neither do you. Who can tell what will happen?"

"I'm pretty sure I won't be moving to Paris. After all, I don't think they have a big need for deputy sheriffs."

"Is that all you're trained to do?"

"'Fraid so. I majored in law enforcement back in

Colorado. My minor was business, but I don't think I have much talent in that area."

"You seem better suited to ranching than anything else."

Harry shook his head. "I don't know much about that, either. John knows tons more than me. But I can ride a horse and chase a few cows, so I could probably work as a cowhand. I like being a deputy sheriff here, however."

"But you can't get promoted to sheriff. Mike is young and he's not going anywhere."

"I know," Harry said. "I wouldn't want him to leave. He's good for Rawhide."

"Well, Caro certainly doesn't want him to go move away. If he left, she'd go with him and the whole town would protest."

Harry laughed.

"It doesn't bother you that you can't be promoted?" Melissa pressed.

"No. Mike lets all of us take responsibility. We're happy being deputy sheriffs."

But he could tell Melissa didn't really understand his position. She was a go-getter, career minded, with high ambition. An ambition that had taken her halfway around the world.

When the takeout order was ready, Harry grabbed the sacks and, after Melissa paid the bill, walked her to the hospital.

He held the door open and after a thank-you, goodbye

and a smile, Melissa rushed through it, eager to find out how her mother was doing.

Despite the smile, Harry felt all knotted up. Over breakfast they'd laughed easily, and he was beginning to think they'd made a connection—beyond the physical one that had been there since the night in the bar. Until she brought up their innate differences.

He left her at the hospital and headed over to the Sheriff's Office to work out. That was exactly what he needed to blow off his mood.

"What are you doing here, Harry?" a voice called out as he walked into the Sheriff's Office. "You don't work on Sundays."

"Hi, Wayne. I thought I'd catch up on some things today." Without any small talk, he headed for the workout room.

"Uh, before you go, Harry, I need to tell you something."

"Look, if you're referring to what happened earlier, it's no big deal."

"No, that wasn't it. I wouldn't have said anything if I'd known that was you, but I hadn't heard you'd found a new lady."

Harry squared his shoulders. "What did you need to tell me?"

"Uh, I turned in my resignation earlier this morning."

"You *what?* Why would you do that, Wayne? I thought you were happy here."

"I am! I mean, I was. But my wife's mother died and she says we need to go to Cody to help out her dad."

"And you're willing to do that?"

With a rueful grin, Wayne said, "Yeah. She has to come first, you know? Mike's promised to call the sheriff in Cody and see if he'll consider me for the first opening they have."

"I bet they will. Mike's made a good reputation for himself and our department since he's been here." Harry crossed over to the desk where Wayne was sitting and offered his hand. "I'll miss you, Wayne. It's been good working with you."

"You've taught me a lot, Harry. It's not just Mike. You've been a real help. I'll miss everyone here. I feel like I'm letting down the team."

"No, you're right, Wayne. The wife has to come first." After he said that, Harry moved toward the workout facility, eager to start feeling those endorphins.

"You don't have to work today, Harry. Consider it my farewell gift."

"Naw, I'll work. You might need some extra time helping your wife pack up." He closed the door behind him before Wayne could argue. Harry figured he needed the discipline that the job brought to him. It would help keep thoughts of Melissa at bay.

If anything could.

Chapter Six

"All I hear is 'Harry this' and 'Harry that.' I guess I owe him a debt of gratitude for taking care of you all."

Camille smiled at her family, gathered on both sides of her bed. They'd been here when she woke up, and their faces were a blessed sight, one that had brought tears to her eyes.

"We were worried about you," Griff explained. "I guess we needed Harry's level head." He took his wife's hand.

"He reminded us to eat." Melissa added.

"And he kept us from having a fight right there in the waiting room," John stated.

Immediately Melissa and Griff turned to glare at him, and Camille noticed his deer-in-the-headlights look.

"Fight? You almost had a fight? What about?" she demanded.

"It was nothing, Mom," Melissa insisted.

"Yeah, honey, it was just the tension," Griff said hurriedly.

Camille looked at her son. She could always get information out of him. "John?"

"Uh, yeah, Mom, it was just the tension."

"Children, I need to speak to your father alone," Camille said calmly, with a smile.

"I don't think—"

She cut off her husband with another plea to her children.

"We'll see you later, Mom," John said, bending to kiss her cheek.

Melissa sent her father an apologetic look and followed her brother out of the room.

Griff gave his wife a smile. "Now, honey, there's nothing to worry about."

"I hope not, dear, but I would guess it was one of two things. Either you were pressing Melissa about Harry, or you were pressing her about returning home. And I won't have either one occurring. Do you hear me?"

"Sweetheart, it's only right that a daughter be there for her mother," Griff stated, his voice filled with righteous indignation.

"She is here for me right now, isn't she? That doesn't mean she has to give up her life in France. She's an adult and she gets to make her own choices. I don't want you mentioning that subject to her ever again!"

"But what if you get sick again?"

Camille saw the fear on his face, but she gave him a soulful look. "You mean you wouldn't take care of me?"

"Of course I would, sweetheart! I'll always be here for you!"

"Good. Then we don't have to worry about what Melissa does, do we? Because I'll always be here for you, too."

Griff leaned over to kiss her. "You're right, honey. I guess it was the fear that got to me. I shouldn't have said anything. Anyway, Harry saw that both Melissa and I needed a breather, so he took her to get lunch for us. He was a good friend this morning."

"But you didn't push Harry on her, did you?"

"Nope. I wasn't thinking that clearly." He laughed. "I swear it was Harry's idea. And Melissa went with him without fussing. She seemed okay when she came back, didn't she?"

"Yes, she did. You've all been wonderful, dear."

"We're trying, honey."

"Now, I want the three of you to go home. The nurses will take care of me, but the ranch needs you, especially in this weather."

"Let Melissa stay with you, and John and I will go. I don't want you here alone."

"All right. But take Melissa home so she can pack a bag, then bring her back. I don't think she's used to driving in this much snow."

"You've got a deal, sweetheart." He kissed her again and headed for the waiting room.

After Griff announced that they were going home,

Melissa stepped forward. "I'll stay here with Mom. She shouldn't be left alone."

"That's what I told her, honey. She's going to have a nap while I take you home to pack a bag. I'll have you back here within the hour."

And he was true to his word, pulling up at the hospital forty-five minutes later. "Take good care of your mother," he said to her.

"I will, Dad, I promise."

"Oh, and about that almost-fight we had, that won't happen again. You're right, you're an adult. You get to make your own decisions, no matter what I think about them."

Melissa drew a deep breath. "Thank you, Dad."

"I'm going to drop by the Sheriff's Office and thank Harry again. Any message you want me to take him?"

"No, thank you."

"Okay, then. I'll see you in the morning."

Melissa appreciated her father's apology, but was a little suspicious about his offer to deliver a message to Harry. Maybe she'd check with Harry later, when her dad had gone home.

She found her mother still sleeping, so she took out a pad and pencil and began sketching ideas for new jewelry she might want to make. Especially if she started her own line here in America.

She had forced that idea from her mind while she dealt with the question of her mother's health. Now she could consider her options.

Her opinion didn't change, however. She had learned a great deal from Monsieur Jalbert, but she was tiring of his iron-fisted control. She thought she would enjoy being her own boss. Even if she never got rich from designing jewelry, she didn't have to worry about money. Her father had continued to manage both her and her brother's sizable accounts, established by their grandfather long ago.

Melissa flipped to a new page of her pad and began drafting a letter to her boss, explaining that she wouldn't be renewing her contract and thanking him for all he had taught her. She kept her unhappiness with him to herself. She wouldn't send such a letter until she knew when she would be returning to Paris to pack. But she would be sending it. As for where she'd go to start her business, she wasn't sure. But she had some time now to think and plan.

Meanwhile no one else needed to know her decision. Especially not Harry Gowan. She was enjoying his goodbye kisses too much to take away his reason for them. A wicked smile crossed her lips at the thought.

"What are you thinking about, young lady?" her mother asked softly.

"Mom, when did you wake up?"

"Just in time to see that interesting smile. You haven't answered my question."

"Oh, I've been sketching designs I might want to make. What do you think of this one?" Melissa asked, hoping to distract her. She showed her a necklace.

"I like it. What's the center stone?"

"Mmm, I was thinking an opal, but a citrine might look good, too. I could make it with both stones."

"I might be interested in buying one of those."

"Mom, you don't have to buy anything I make. I think an opal would look best on you. I'll make it for you for Christmas."

"I think your father should buy it for me. It might make up for his trying to force you to stay."

Melissa leaned over to kiss her mother's cheek. "He's already apologized, Mom. I knew it was because you talked to him, but I still appreciated it."

"Good for him."

"Have they gotten you out of bed yet? Caro said they would."

"No, but I went to sleep after lunch. Probably—"

Camille stopped speaking as the door to her room opened and a nurse came in.

"Right on cue," she muttered.

"You were expecting me?" the nurse called cheerfully.

"My daughter was asking if you'd gotten me out of bed yet. I said you hadn't had time because I went to sleep after lunch."

"Then I *am* right on cue. Dr. Randall said we should get you up before you went to bed tonight. It's going to be hard for you, but it'll make it easier in the morning. Okay?"

"Yes, of course."

"Melissa, do you want to stay? If you have trouble watching your mom struggle—"

"No, I won't. I need to be here so I'll know how to help her when she gets home."

"Good for you. Okay, Camille, let's give it a try. Sit up and slide your legs over the side of the bed."

Camille, grimacing, did as she was told.

"Okay. Now I'm going to help you stand. Let me do the work. Then we'll walk."

Melissa stood back and watched as the nurse helped her mother take about six steps. Then they turned and walked back to the bed.

"Good job, Camille."

"Th-thank you," she muttered.

"I'm going to give you another pain pill now," the nurse said. "You've earned it."

Melissa moved closer and held her mother's hand after she took the medication. Slowly, Camille relaxed, and soon fell asleep.

After a moment, when she was sure her mother was sound asleep, Melissa stepped out to the nurse's desk. "My mom went to sleep after she took her pain pill." She nodded over her shoulder toward the room. "If she wakes up before I get back, can you tell her I stepped out for just a minute?"

"Will do," the nurse replied.

Melissa pulled on her coat and went out into the brisk air and sunshine. She walked quickly down the sidewalk until she reached the Sheriff's Office.

Inside, she found Harry alone. "Hi, Harry," she said softly.

He jumped up before she finished speaking. "Melissa! Is everything all right? Your mother—"

"She's fine. She's sleeping now. I just wanted to be sure— That is, my dad said he was coming to see you, and asked if he could deliver a message from me. I said no, but I wasn't sure I could trust him."

Harry looked puzzled. "No, he didn't say anything about a message. What was it?"

"There wasn't any message. I was just afraid he might make up something. You know, in a matchmaking effort."

"No, I think he's given up on that idea."

She walked over and sat on the edge of his desk. "Really?"

"Yeah. He thanked me for interrupting your argument and getting you out of there. He said he'd been wrong to start it. He even said he realized you had to make your own decisions."

"Don't give him too much credit. Mom read him the riot act after John mentioned that we almost had a fight."

"I see. Well, it must make you feel good to know he'll accept your decision if you decide to go back to France."

"If?"

"I thought maybe you'd reconsidered."

"I have to go back to France." To pack up her belongings, but she wasn't revealing that decision to Harry. Especially since she wasn't returning to Rawhide to live.

"Damn, lady, you've got to stop telling me that."

Since he didn't immediately take her in his arms, she

decided he needed a little more persuasion. "Why? Are you going to kiss me goodbye again?"

"I guess I might as well, since you're going." He stood and tugged her into his arms for another gut-wrenching kiss. She wrapped her arms around his neck and didn't let him pull away. He deepened the kiss and she felt the magic all the way to her toes. No one man could kiss the way Harry Gowan could. In fact, she felt as if she'd never been kissed before. Until now.

They were so caught up in the moment, neither of them heard the door open.

"Harry, I— Harry?"

Harry almost dropped Melissa as he realized his partner had walked in on them, but caught her as she started to stumble. Then, with great decorum, he set her away from him.

"Uh, Steve, is there anything to report?"

"No, nothing at all," Steve said, his eyes wide as he stared at them.

"Melissa just…uh, stopped off to tell me her mother is doing well."

"Good to hear."

They all stood there, unease and embarrassment filling the space between them. Finally, Melissa moved toward the door. "I'd better get back to the hospital," she said, smiling over her shoulder at Harry.

He immediately moved after her, catching up with her at the door. "I'll see you in the morning."

"You will?" She couldn't help the jump her heart made.

"Yeah. I'll come take you to breakfast."

"Okay."

A smile played about her lips as she walked out. She'd hoped Harry would extend an invitation if she came to see him.

Mission accomplished.

"HARRY, I'M SORRY I interrupted you, but—I didn't know you and Melissa were— I mean, you didn't seem very friendly the other day when she came into the workout facility."

"She didn't actually come in, Steve. She just opened the door."

"Well, yeah, you seemed just as upset as me when she did that."

"It doesn't matter. She's going back to France after the holidays."

"But, Harry—"

"Let it go, Steve!"

"Okay." He walked to his desk, his head bent. "Did you hear about Wayne?"

"Yeah, he told me when I came in." Harry sat back down and started working on the weekly schedule again.

Steve was silent for several minutes, and Harry thought he'd discouraged any further conversation. He was wrong.

"Would you do that?"

"Do what?"

"Give up your job just because your wife said to."

"Like Wayne said, his first allegiance is to his wife."

"So you'd do the same thing?"

"I'm not married, Steve. You know that."

"I know, but if you got married."

Harry shook his head. "I'm not, so I'm not going to speculate on it. But if you are, your prime allegiance should go to your wife."

More silence.

Harry again drew a deep breath, glad he'd ended that conversation. But he was wrong again.

"My wife wants us to move back to Denver to be with her parents."

Harry looked up. "Are they in poor health?"

"No. Her father goes out and plays golf every day, and her mother volunteers all over town. They're perfectly happy."

"Then why does she want to go back?"

"She's spoiled. She thinks she can always get her way."

"Well, if you're going to give in to her, Steve, talk her into waiting until we find someone to take Wayne's place."

Steve shook his head. "Heck, I'm not giving in. She agreed to move here with me when I got the job. She can't change her mind now."

"Your decision, Steve, but remember what I said."

"I know."

"I need to finish the schedule now. We're all going to have to take up the slack until we find someone new."

"Does the sheriff have a waiting list?"

"I haven't talked to him about it."

"Okay. I'll let you work now. Maybe I'd better take another walk around town."

"Good idea," Harry agreed, keeping his head down. But when the door closed behind Steve, he slumped back in his chair. He'd tried to keep Melissa out of his mind while he was talking to his partner, but she was still firmly planted there. How could he focus on anything else when he'd just held her in his arms?

He thought he had better self-discipline than he'd demonstrated so far. If he wasn't careful, people were going to start talking about him and Melissa. After she went back to France, he'd have to deal with sympathetic smiles and pats on his back, people trying to let him know that they all felt for him.

It might be more than he could bear.

But Melissa leaving was definitely more than he could bear if he didn't keep his distance from her from now on.

And, damn it, he'd promised to take her to breakfast in the morning!

What was wrong with him?

Harry rubbed his face. It was too late to think about canceling his breakfast date. He wouldn't do that to Melissa. Tomorrow, he'd have to tell her he'd be avoiding her from then on.

He could do that, right? He could look into those big blue eyes, study those pouty lips and tell her he wouldn't be kissing her goodbye anymore, couldn't he?

He shook his head, unconsciously giving himself his answer. Lord have mercy, he didn't know.

Chapter Seven

Harry was finally hard at work—after an hour of alternately castigating himself and searching his soul—when the door opened again.

He was afraid to look up this time.

"Harry, you're just the man I wanted to see."

The words were ones he longed to hear, but the speaker was Mike Davis.

"Hey, Sheriff, working double time?" he asked, finally letting himself glance up.

"I wanted to talk to you for a few minutes. Get your opinion on something."

"I was just making out the schedule now." Harry held out the piece of paper he'd been working on.

Mike pulled out a chair beside Harry's desk. "Good. But actually, I wanted to talk to you about a couple of men I think might take Wayne's place."

"You got someone in mind?"

"Yeah. One of them is Trevor Kenyon. He's a deputy

in Buffalo. He's mentioned to me several times that he'd like to move back to Rawhide. His folks are from here."

"Right, I remember him. Good looking guy." Harry stopped himself. Rawhide didn't need a handsome deputy. Unless... "He's married, right?"

"Yeah. Why would that matter?"

Damn it, was he losing his mind? "Uh, it doesn't, really. I've just heard that married men were more settled."

Mike rolled his eyes. "You're not married, Harry, and you're my best deputy."

"Thanks, Mike. But, as a rule, I mean—"

Mike looked at him through narrowed eyes. "Are you trying to tell me you've got your eye on a young lady and you don't want any competition?"

"No! No, that's not what I meant at all."

"Good, 'cause I've been wondering. I've heard rumors, you know."

"What kind of rumors?" Harry asked sharply.

Mike smiled. "I heard you're interested in a Randall lady."

"She's leaving. She's going back to France." He regretted his response at once because it only confirmed the rumors.

"Are you sure? You're usually pretty persuasive."

"I'm not trying to be. She has to want to stay here on her own. It won't work any other way."

Mike gave him a sympathetic look. "I'm sorry, Harry. I'd hoped for better for you. These Randall women are hard to forget."

"Yeah, even if they live in France."

"Well, Trev definitely wouldn't be a threat. The other man I was thinking about is Dale Henry. He's on the Cody staff. We could make a simple switch and ensure Wayne a job there."

"Is Dale married?"

"No, he's not." Mike waited for Harry's response.

With a sigh, he said, "I'd have to vote for the switch with the Cody sheriff, to give Wayne a job there. He's been really good for us. He deserves the job."

Mike smiled. "I appreciate the sacrifice, Harry. I know Wayne will, too."

"It's not really a sacrifice. Like I said, she's going back to France anyway."

"Even if she were to stay here, I don't think anyone could knock you out of the running, Harry. The whole town is behind you."

"No one knows, Mike!"

"Aw, come on, Harry, you know this community better than that. You kissed the woman on a downtown street!"

"There wasn't anyone around, I swear!"

"Not when you started kissing, Harry, but by the time you finished, Wayne wasn't the only one who saw you."

"Damn!"

Mike laughed. "You've got to look for 'em around every corner, boy. Folks love to talk about our love lives. When Caro and I were dating, they knew our every move."

"I remember. But I thought *I'd* been discreet."

"Yeah, I thought so, too. And I wasn't just kissing her. It's a wonder Jake didn't throw a punch my way."

"Melissa swears her dad is trying to play match-maker for the two of us."

Mike rubbed the back of his neck. "Could be. The Randalls seem to think they can maneuver their daughters that way."

"Was Jake trying to match up the two of you?"

"Yeah, I guess so. But I didn't put any stock in it."

"Yeah, me neither," Harry said glumly.

Mike stood and slapped his friend on his shoulder. "Maybe things will work out, Harry. I'll keep my fingers crossed for you. And thanks for making the right decision about Wayne."

"Sure, boss. No problem."

No. No problem. Because he figured Melissa would be back in France before Dale could move to Rawhide.

MIKE ENTERED the small house on one of the few back streets of Rawhide. The place still looked the same as it had the first time he'd entered it, to arrest the woman inside for breaking and entering.

Then he'd married her.

"Honey, is that you?" Caroline called.

Before he could answer, she came into the room, carrying their baby. Their oldest son came running after his mother.

"Well, this is a fine welcome." He bent over to kiss his

wife, then his baby, Jake. Then he opened his arms to his four-year-old son, Samuel. "How is everyone?" he asked.

"We're fine. Did you visit with Harry?"

"Yeah, he voted for the switch so Wayne could have a job. I figured he would, but he had to make a hard choice."

"He doesn't like the new man?"

"He's never met him. But he asked if he was married."

"Is he?"

"No."

Caroline eyed her husband. "You're trying to tell me something, but you're just going to have to come out with it. I'm not catching on."

Mike settled on the sofa and set his son on his feet. "Go play, Sam. I need to talk to Mama."

Caroline joined him on the sofa. "Okay, what?"

"Harry's falling for someone."

"Really? That's great!" Caroline said with a big smile. Harry was a favorite of hers.

"No, not so great. He's falling for a Randall."

"A Randall? But there aren't any— Melissa! That's why he was in the waiting room this morning."

"Probably. It's all over town that someone saw him kissing her on the street this morning."

"That wasn't too discreet."

"That's the funny part. He thought he was being discreet!"

Caroline laughed. "In Rawhide?"

"Honey, can't you talk to her?"

Caroline stopped laughing. "About what?"

"Staying here."

"No, I can't, and I can't believe Harry would want me to."

Mike sighed. "All right, you're on the same page with Harry."

"You mean he doesn't want me to talk to Melissa?"

"I never said he did. You just assumed—"

She punched him in his gut. "Mike Davis, you tried to sucker me!"

"Hey, that's not fair. I was just trying to get some help for Harry. I want him to be happy."

Caroline moved closer, leaning into her husband's arms. "I want that for him, too. But Melissa lives in France. She's only here for a visit."

"He knows."

"If she ever asks my opinion, I'll encourage her, but it has to be her decision."

"That's what Harry said, too."

"Now that we've had our little chat, go change your son's diaper while I start fixing dinner."

"Yes, ma'am. Come on, shorty."

MELISSA AND HER MOTHER spent the evening chatting about their lives and their loved ones. It was a time Melissa cherished. She even considered telling her Mom about her decision. But she didn't. Not because she couldn't trust her; she knew she could. But she feared her mother would think her illness had forced the decision.

It hadn't.

Melissa was ready for the change. For starting her own company here in the U.S. For returning to her homeland. Maybe even for visiting her hometown a lot more often.

But Harry wouldn't kiss her then, she thought, and was stunned by the feeling of loss that consumed her.

Whoa! She hadn't intended to let things go so far. Maybe she should back off the idea of continuing the kissing game with Harry. He certainly was a good kisser. No doubt about that. But she hadn't thought a few kisses could sway her.

Melissa finally admitted that she didn't want to back away from Harry. She was enjoying the game they were playing almost as much as the kisses she received. Even if she moved to New York, they could still kiss occasionally, couldn't they? After all, she'd come home frequently...right?

When a nurse brought her evening pills, Camille downed them promptly with a glass of water. After the nurse left the room, Camille said, "She's cute, isn't she?"

"Yes. I don't think I know her. Did she move here after I left?"

"Yes, Betsy replaced a nurse Harry used to date. But they broke up and she married someone else. There's been talk that Harry might be interested in this lady."

"Oh, really?" *He'd better not be!* Melissa thought. After all, he was kissing her, wasn't he? Surely he wasn't two-timing her. But it gave her food for thought. When she left, someone else might move in on Harry. Melissa wouldn't like that.

So what should she do? Back away, leaving him ripe for the picking? No, she didn't think so. She'd keep playing the game as long as Harry was willing.

She went to sleep that evening with a smile on her lips.

THE FIRST THING Melissa did the next morning was inform the nurse she wouldn't need breakfast ordered for her. Then she woke her mother, helped her wash up, and got her ready for her meal.

"The nurse said she'd be in after breakfast to get you up to walk again. She said you did so well yesterday that today would be a lot easier for you."

Camille sighed. "I hope so."

"And while you're walking, I'm going to go to the café with Harry. He offered yesterday to buy me breakfast."

"Yesterday morning?" Camille asked innocently, keeping an eye on her daughter.

With her cheeks flushed, Melissa looked away and said, "Uh, no, I saw him later, when you were napping."

"Oh. Well, that's nice."

Melissa breathed a sigh of relief. She'd worried about mentioning her breakfast date. Her father would've made a big deal about it. Thankfully, her mother didn't react that way.

Melissa had just finished clearing her mom's tray when the nurse came in. "Melissa, Harry's in the waiting room."

"Oh, thank you." She checked to be sure her mother had everything she would need at hand. "I should be back in an hour, Mom."

"Take your time. I'll probably go to sleep after I do my walking."

Melissa kissed her cheek and left the room, a big smile on her face.

"Your daughter certainly seems happy," the nurse said.

"Yes, I think so, too."

After Camille did her requisite walking, moving out into the hall and then returning to her bed, the nurse offered another pain pill.

"I don't think I need it this morning," she stated.

"Well, let me know if you change your mind. We don't want you to suffer."

"All right."

After the nurse left, Camille gradually let her muscles relax. Just as she was completely comfortable, the door opened and her husband entered the room.

He gave her a good-morning kiss, then looked around with a frown. "Where's Melissa?"

"She's gone to breakfast."

"I thought they'd order her food. Haven't you eaten?"

"Yes, and I've done my walking."

"Walking? This early?"

"Yes, I walked out into the hallway and back. With the nurse's help."

"That's terrific, honey!" He gave her another kiss. "When will Melissa be back?"

"I don't know. I told her to take her time."

"Well, yeah, of course, but—"

"She's with Harry."

Suddenly Griff stopped complaining. "She is? How did you manage that?"

"I didn't do anything. Well, not much."

"And you complained about me matchmaking!"

"I wasn't matchmaking. I just mentioned that Harry might have an interest in one of the pretty nurses."

Griff sat down on the side of his wife's bed. "You're the best, sweetheart. Much more subtle than me."

Camille laughed. "It wouldn't take much to be more subtle than you, dear."

"ARE YOU GOING TO HAVE French toast again?" Harry asked, eyeing the woman across the table from him.

"Why, yes, if you don't mind."

"No, I don't mind, Melissa. I enjoyed watching you eat it yesterday."

"And the fact that I gave you a bite?"

"Yeah. I'm hoping for another one today." He listened with pleasure as she laughed.

"How's your mom this morning?"

"She's doing very well. She should be able to go home in a couple of days."

"A good thing you're here, isn't it?"

"Yes," Melissa agreed warily. "You're not going to tell me it's a reason I shouldn't go back to France, are you?"

Harry gave her a direct look. "No, I'm not going to tell you that, and I don't think your mother will, either."

"Thank you. No, she won't."

"I would ask you if you're still going back to France,

but I can't do anything about it anyway. Besides, we've already caused enough talk."

Melissa's head snapped up. "Talk? What do you mean?"

"Mike said someone saw us on the street yesterday when I was kissing you." He flexed his jaw. "I didn't think anyone was around."

"Oh. So you wouldn't have kissed me if you'd known?"

"Damn it, Melissa, everyone's going to feel sorry for me when you leave!"

"Are you ready to order?" a waitress asked, suddenly appearing at their table.

"Yes, I'll have the French toast, please." Melissa looked at Harry, a challenge in her eyes.

"I'll have the number-two breakfast, please," he said, folding his menu and handing it to the waitress. Melissa hurriedly did the same.

"I didn't realize I was making you an object of pity just by letting you kiss me!" she whispered as soon as the waitress moved away.

"I'm not complaining. I just didn't intend for anyone to see us. I thought you should know."

"I think I'll survive," she told him, letting her irritation show.

"Oh, really? Even if your dad hears the rumors?"

Harry felt guilty for his remark when Melissa paled.

"Oh, no! I hadn't realized— Maybe he won't hear."

"Yeah, right. As Mike said, you know how much townsfolk around here gossip."

Melissa groaned. "Dad's going to think he's won."

"Not if you keep telling him you're moving back to France. Surely he won't believe a simple kiss is going to keep you here."

She lifted her chin. "No, I guess not."

The waitress brought their food, but neither of them ate with any appetite. In fact, all enjoyment of their breakfast date seemed to have fled.

After a few minutes, having stirred the food around on their plates, they abandoned the effort. Harry paid the bill and then escorted her back to the hospital. He walked with her into the waiting room, which was empty.

She turned to stare at him. "Well, I guess this is goodbye."

He knew what she was doing. And he'd resolved not to rise to the bait. But he couldn't pass up one last chance to taste those delectable lips, to hold her body against his. "Then I'd better kiss you goodbye." He pulled her into his arms.

Melissa went willingly. After all, she'd practically begged him to kiss her again. She knew what those words did to him.

Those lips he couldn't refuse clung to his, and her arms held him close. But he wanted to be closer. He hugged her tightly against him, running his hands up and down her back. He slanted his mouth over hers to take the kiss deeper. She met him at every turn.

"Melissa! Harry! Have you lost all sense of decency? Anyone could walk in on you!"

At the sound of Griff's voice they broke apart, but Harry kept his gaze on Melissa rather than look at her father. Just in case she wanted to ignore that sense of decency and come back into his arms.

"Dad!" Melissa exclaimed. "What are you doing here?"

"I came to see your mom. Didn't you expect me?"

"I—I—Yes, of course."

"I'm not complaining if you and Harry are…involved, but I'd rather everyone in town didn't know that."

"You're not the only one," Harry muttered, and then regretted his words as the older man glared at him. "I'm sorry, Griff. We thought we were alone."

"We were until you interrupted us!" Melissa pointed out, as if what had happened was her father's fault.

"This is a public waiting room, Melissa. Anyone could've come in. Some of the ladies are planning on visiting your mother today. What if they'd walked in?"

"Then I suppose I would've been a little embarrassed," Melissa muttered.

"A little?" Griff asked in outrage.

"We weren't making love, Dad! We were just kissing!"

"I'm not so sure of that!" Griff growled, staring at Harry.

Harry stepped forward. "If we went beyond kissing, I'm the one responsible, not Melissa. Take out your anger on me, Griff."

"I'm just saying you should be more careful," he said in a loud voice.

"I realize that," Harry muttered, his face turning red.

A nurse stepped into the room. "Mrs. Randall said you can all come in." She held the door open for them.

They all looked at each other. Griff said softly, "Not a word."

The other two nodded and followed him back to Camille's room.

"Mom, how did the walking go?"

"Never mind my walking. What were the three of you arguing about out there? Half the hospital could hear you!" Camille exclaimed, staring from one to the other.

"Um, I was complaining that Melissa took too long at breakfast," Griff said cajolingly.

Camille gave him a stern look. "Don't lie to me, Griffin Randall. I know better than that."

"Really, Mom, it was nothing," Melissa said, though it was evident her words didn't appease her mother.

"Look, I have to be here. The least you can do is not make it so embarrassing for me, having my family arguing."

"It's my fault, Camille," Harry said quietly. "I was kissing Melissa and your husband walked in on us."

Camille stared at her husband and daughter. "That's all? You raised such a commotion over a simple kiss?"

Griff protested. "It didn't look that simple to me. I thought they were headed to the nearest bed!"

"And you of all people were opposed? When our son was born 'prematurely' and weighed eight pounds, five ounces?"

"Mom!" Melissa exclaimed.

"Camille, must you spread that information around?"

"Why not? You were doing the same thing to Melissa, weren't you?"

Chapter Eight

After Griff and Harry had withdrawn, Melissa apologized to her mother again.

"Don't worry about it, dear. I blame your father."

"I should bear part of the blame, Mom. By the way, if there's anything I can do to help you, I'll be glad to do it."

"What's today's date?"

Melissa frowned, then replied, "It's the eighth of November.

"So Thanksgiving is just a little over two weeks from now?"

"That's right. Why?"

"Well, if I can't make my share of Thanksgiving dinner, I'll need you to make it for me."

"What's your share?"

"Dessert."

"Of course I can do that."

"Well, I'm not sure. It's going to be something you've never made before."

"What could that be?" Melissa asked with a laugh. She was an experienced cook, after all.

"Red's chocolate cake."

Melissa stared at Camille. "What's wrong with Red?"

"He's fine, though he and Mildred are complaining because you haven't been out to see them."

"Oh, I should've thought of that. But your surgery distracted me."

"They understand. But as soon as I've recovered somewhat, you'd better plan a trip out to the ranch."

"Definitely." She'd like nothing better than to go visit the domestic couple who had become family to not only Uncle Jake and his brothers, but to all the Randalls. "But how will you make his chocolate cake? No one knows the recipe."

"He's given it to all of us second generation ladies."

"Are you sure he's all right?"

"Of course he is, honey. I would've told you if something was wrong with Red. But, you know, he's getting up in years and he's decided to share his secret now. He told us we could pass it on when our daughters marry."

"But that means I'm the only one of my generation who doesn't have it."

"And Mildred's cinnamon bun recipe, too."

"Wow, talk about incentive! Why didn't you tell me earlier?"

"Do you think I wanted you to marry a Frenchman and have my grandbabies over there?"

Melissa didn't let herself dwell too long on her mother's remark. "Oh, Mom, cut it out."

"I would've accepted it if you'd fallen in love on your own, but I wasn't going to offer any incentives."

Melissa needed to change the subject. "But you'll have to let me see the recipe if you don't feel up to making the cake."

"Yes, but you'll have to promise not to tell Red you've already seen it." Her mother winked at her.

"Okay, I promise."

"Good. Then I don't have to worry."

"You certainly don't. Unless I have to break your leg to ensure that you can't make the cake," Melissa teased.

Camille laughed, but before she could respond, the door opened and two of Melissa's aunts entered. "Aunt Megan, Aunt B.J., hello."

B.J. leaned over to Megan. "You know, I think that sounds like Melissa, but I'm sure if she was back she would've been out to see us before now."

"I would have thought so," Megan agreed, grinning at Melissa.

She went over to her aunts and hugged them. "I'm sorry, you two. I've been busy."

"So we heard," B.J. assured her as she and Megan went directly to Camille's side. "How are you, love?"

"Actually, I'm doing fairly well. I walked out in the hallway this morning, and my nurse says tomorrow I'll be able to walk all alone."

The ladies praised her and then started to gossip

about the family. Fortunately, much to Melissa's relief, they said nothing about her and Harry.

"Dear, would you go get us all some drinks from the vending machine?" Camille eventually asked her.

"Sure. What would you like?"

They all gave her their preferences. As soon as she left the room, Megan said, "I guess you're hearing all the gossip about her and Harry, aren't you?"

"Maybe not all of it, but Griff threw a fit in the waiting room earlier. Seems he walked in on the pair of them kissing."

"Well, the rumors started yesterday when they were seen kissing on the sidewalk around ten in the morning. Everyone figured it must be serious to be going on that early in the day," B.J. said.

"Can you believe Griff was making such a scene? I pointed out to him that, since our son was born a month early, weighing as much as he did, Griff didn't have much room to complain."

The ladies were all laughing as Melissa came back in, carrying cans of soda.

"Oh, thank you, Melissa." B.J. opened her drink at once and took a long sip. "My throat gets so dry in winter."

"Mine, too," Megan agreed. "Oh, Melissa, did you make those earrings you're wearing?" She leaned forward to examine them.

Melissa had intended asking them what was so funny, but her aunt's interest in her jewelry distracted her. "Yes, I did. I made these last year."

"Ooh, I love them. They look old-fashioned, yet totally chic!"

"That was the effect I was hoping to achieve," Melissa said with a smile.

"Did you get my name for Christmas?" Megan asked hopefully.

"Oh, I forgot to ask Mom."

"I know whose name she got," Camille said, "but it's supposed to be a secret."

B.J. tried convincing her otherwise. "Oh, come on, Camille. It's just the kids who aren't supposed to know."

"Fine," she said, "but you're not going to be happy about it. She got Josh."

The two aunts looked disappointed.

"See? I told you," Camille said with a sigh.

"I don't suppose you'd want to find out who has my name and switch with them?" Megan asked.

"Hey, it should be for my name. After all, Josh is my son," B.J. pointed out.

"Yeah, but— You know, I bet I could sell those in my store. Is there any way I could do that?" Megan asked.

Her aunt's shop, where she sold antiques and high-end items, would be a perfect venue for her jewelery. But… "I'm afraid not. I'm under contract with a French jewelery designer," Melissa murmured.

"Rats!"

"Do you really think you could sell some here?" she asked.

"Probably not too many if they all looked alike, but

I could take a sampling and sell some, especially right before Christmas."

"Well, maybe one day. I'll keep it in mind for the future."

"Does that mean you're thinking of returning to Rawhide?" B.J. asked.

"No, but I'm thinking about changing companies."

"I didn't know that, dear," Camille said. "You hadn't mentioned it."

"I've been a little unhappy with Monsieur Jalbert for a few months. It's a decision that is slowly evolving."

"Will you have to move your workshop?" Megan asked.

"Perhaps. I'll have to look into that when I return to France."

After chatting a few minutes more, the ladies left, just as a nurse brought in lunch.

"Perfect timing," Camille said, smiling at the woman.

But when she saw the burger and fries that awaited her, she sighed. "I'm eager to get home for so many reasons. But a home-cooked meal probably tops the list."

HARRY HAD JUST SAT DOWN at his desk on Tuesday when Wayne came in. The man was downright ecstatic. "Harry, I wanted to thank you. Mike said you voted to do the switch so I could have a job right away. I can't thank you enough."

"You deserve it, Wayne. You've worked well for us

here. I'm sure the sheriff in Cody will realize what a great deputy he's getting. When are you reporting?"

"Monday morning. We won't be moved by then, but my wife said she'd stay here until the movers can work us in. It shouldn't be more than a couple of days after that. We're both excited about me having a job right off."

"Monday? Is—is Dale reporting here on Monday?"

"Yeah. That was the deal. But he's not married, so he doesn't have that much to bring with him."

Harry didn't need that reminder of Dale's bachelor status. "Where is he going to live?"

"I think Mike said he talked to Russ, who's got an opening in one of his apartments above the office."

"I see."

"Mike's giving me the rest of the week off so I can help my wife pack. I just wanted to say thank-you. And anytime you come to Cody, just let me know. We'll have a place for you."

"Thanks, Wayne. I'll remember that."

With a beaming smile, Wayne left the office. Once he was gone, Harry buried his face in his hands. Dale Henry would be here on Monday. It was a wonder he wasn't going to be here tomorrow!

Harry hoped Camille would be going home tomorrow, or Thursday at the latest, to get Melissa out of town. He was afraid she'd fall for anyone in a uniform. Was it just his luck that he'd been the only single guy on the force?

Suddenly he raised his head. Of course. He should've thought of this idea before. What was the name of that new nurse over at the hospital? His friends had given him her name awhile back, thinking he might be interested because he'd dated Susan, her predecessor, a few years ago. Was it Betsy? Yes, that was it. He could introduce Dale to her. The new deputy would probably be so grateful, he wouldn't be looking for anyone else.

That's what Harry would do. He'd introduce him to Betsy.

Of course, that might be hard, since he hadn't met Betsy yet himself. Maybe Mike would want Dale to get his blood type on record, and Harry could escort him over to the clinic and request Betsy.

"Hey, Harry," Mike called, walking into the office. "Did Wayne tell you the good news?"

"That he starts his job next Monday? Yeah, he was just in here."

"Good. Dale is supposed to be here then, too. I just wanted to make sure you knew, in case he comes in early, that I've rented Russ's upstairs apartment, the one on the north side, for Dale. If you're in the office when he gets here, can you take him over there and introduce him to Russ?"

"Sure. But you don't expect him before Monday, do you?"

"I just know if I was him and didn't have a lot of personal stuff, I'd want to get here early and settle in. After all, he doesn't have a wife to do that stuff for him."

Why did everyone have to remind him of that? Harry wondered. "I don't think Caro would like to hear you talking about wives like that," he teased.

Mike laughed. "Yeah, you're probably right. Anyway, you're okay with that?"

"Sure, boss. I can handle it."

"Thanks, Harry. I'll be watching the county road tonight, so I'm going home now to take a nap. If you haven't seen me by dark, call the house and wake me up."

"Okay. But what about the kids?"

"B.J. came in to see Camille this morning, and picked the kids up to take them out to the ranch for the night."

"I bet you're sorry you're going to be working tonight."

"Yeah, but that's my job."

Mike strolled out of the office, and Harry couldn't help smiling. Mike and Caro still acted like they were on their honeymoon, even though they'd been married almost five years now. He hoped, if he ever married, his life would be just like Mike's.

It would be if he married Melissa.

He immediately dismissed that thought. She was going back to France. And that would be the end of anything, no matter how many times he kissed her. And it was a good thing, because the more he kissed her the more he lost control. Griff hadn't been far off the mark this morning.

Harry sighed. He needed to get his mind on something else. Such as the schedule. He plugged Dale into work Wayne's shift, then organized the duties for the remaining five deputies and Mike.

By national standards theirs wasn't a big force, but it was large for a town the size of Rawhide. The ranchers in the area were willing to support the office with Mike in charge. Harry thought that was a smart decision.

The afternoon passed with its normal duties and almost no incident that needed a deputy's attention. Except for an argument that started at the general store. Sarah Randall called the office to ask for help, and Steve volunteered immediately.

Because he had messed up once when on duty at the general store, an incident that resulted in Harry being shot, Steve volunteered for anything that came up there. Fortunately, he was better trained now, so Harry let him take care of the call.

Steve was back in the office when the outer door opened and a stranger walked in.

It only took one look for Harry to realize his wish had not been granted. The new man had arrived early.

With a sigh, Harry stood up and stuck out his hand. "You must be Dale Henry."

"Yeah. How did you know?"

"There's just something about a lawman," Harry said with a crooked smile. "I'm Deputy Sheriff Harry Gowan. This is Steve Lawson. Steve, this is Dale Henry. He's replacing Wayne."

Steve shook his hand. "We didn't think you'd be here much before the weekend."

"Well, I didn't have a lot I had to move. I was renting furnished in Cody."

"You don't have any furniture?" Harry asked, surprised.

"No. Is that a problem?"

"Well, just for tonight. The place Mike rented for you doesn't have any, either."

He stepped over to the front door and pointed across the street to the apartment over Russ Randall's accounting office. "We can probably round some things up tomorrow if you're not particular about style. But you're stuck tonight."

"Is there a hotel here?"

"No. Rawhide is too small. But I've got a sofa you can sleep on. It shouldn't be too uncomfortable, if you don't mind."

"No, that'd be great. Thanks."

"I'm about to go to the café and bring back dinner. What would you like to eat?"

"What do they have?"

"Tonight's special is meat loaf and veggies. They usually have pot roast, and there's always hamburgers."

"I'll take the special. How much do I owe you?"

"Sheriff says the city picks up our meals while we're on duty," Steve interjected.

"I'm not exactly on duty yet, am I?"

"Not technically," Harry said with a wry smile, "but you'll be working the twelve-to-nine shift with me and Steve. You get the first meal free."

"Thanks, Harry. Shall I wait here?"

"Yeah. My apartment is just upstairs. After dinner you can go up whenever you want."

"Thanks again. You're being a great host."

"Harry is always great. And he can teach you a lot," Steve stated.

"Dale may be teaching *us,* Steve. We'll have to wait and see." Then Harry left for the café.

Yeah, he was in trouble, all right, he thought as he dodged a truck barreling down the street. Dale Henry was every bit the looker he'd feared.

Was he Melissa's type?

Then again, what woman wouldn't go for a tall, muscular man in uniform?

Yeah, it was Harry's luck. And now he'd gone ahead and offered the man his sofa for the night. But at least he'd be able to keep an eye on the guy.

Harry picked up the dinners at the café and headed back to the Sheriff's Office. He'd just stepped in when he heard Steve on the phone. "I need to speak to Dr. Randall, please."

Harry nodded toward him. "What's up?"

Dale answered. "Steve wanted to call Sheriff Davis and tell him I'd arrived, but he can't locate him. I tried to tell him to wait, but—"

"Hang up the phone, Steve!" Harry rapped out the order.

Too late. Steve greeted Caroline on the line. "Uh, hello, Dr. Randall. Yes, I wanted to know—"

Harry yanked the phone out Steve's hand and put it to his ear. "Caro, just ignore this call. What? Of course we know where Mike is. I forgot to tell Steve. Yes, I'm sure. No, I won't. Sorry to have bothered you."

After hanging up he turned to his partner. "Steve, don't ever do that again," he declared.

"But I thought—"

"If you called Mike and got no answer, you should've stopped there. The sheriff is working late tonight. Now you've worried Caro for no reason."

"Uh, excuse me," Dale interjected from across the room. "He asked to speak to Dr. Randall? Would that be the famous Randall family? I thought he was calling Sheriff Davis's wife."

"He was. Dr. Caroline Randall Davis. She'd gotten her medical degree and begun practicing here in Rawhide before she and Mike got together."

"Lucky guy," Dale muttered, shaking his head.

Harry gave him a sharp look. "Yeah, he is, for all the right reasons, which has nothing to do with their money."

Dale held up his hands. "Sorry, no offense meant."

"None taken. Let's eat."

Harry showed Dale a desk he could sit at, and handed him a foil-wrapped plate with plastic utensils. "Coffee is in the break room. I'll bring you a cup."

As they ate, Harry relaxed a little, thinking he'd

probably come down on Steve a little hard. Until the phone rang. "Sheriff's Office," he answered.

"Harry, it's Caro. I just wanted to be sure you know where Mike is. He didn't tell me and—"

"Caro, he did tell me. He's doing an all-night stakeout. He probably won't see anything, but he felt he needed to do it. I'll check in with him if you want me to."

"No, I don't want you to bother him. I just wanted to be sure he's all right."

"I'm sure. It's all my fault. I figured I'd be in the office my entire shift, but the new guy got here tonight and I went to get dinner. Steve jumped the gun, trying to be efficient. That's all that happened."

"Okay. Shall I tell Mike the new man is here?"

"Sure, that will be fine. He's sleeping on my couch tonight and we'll try to round up some furniture for him tomorrow."

"Oh, good. I'll call the ranch and see what they have to spare."

"Are you sure you don't mind?"

"No, I'll be glad to."

"Thanks, Caro."

"No. Thank you, Harry, for making me feel better."

"Anytime."

He hung up the phone. Desperate for some time to himself, he suggested Steve take Dale on a tour of Rawhide.

They hadn't been gone ten minutes when the phone

rang again. Harry picked it up to hear the unmistakable voice of Melissa Randall.

"Hey there, deputy," she crooned. "How'd you like some company tonight?"

Chapter Nine

Harry's heart began to thud. Was he dreaming this? "Melissa?" he croaked out in a raspy voice. "Is everything all right?"

She giggled softly. "Yes, of course. Mom has dozed off already, and I thought maybe I could come visit you for a while."

"That wouldn't be a good idea, Melissa." It pained him to admit it. "I'm on duty and—"

"When do you get off duty?"

"At nine, but I've got a guest tonight." Damn. Now for sure he disliked Dale Henry.

"A guest? Is it a female?"

"No!" he barked into the phone. Then he tempered his tone. "No, the new deputy sheriff is here with no furniture, so he can't move into the apartment Mike rented for him because he'd have to sleep on the floor. I offered him my sofa tonight."

"Oh."

"Why did you think it might be a female? Do you

think I go around kissing a lot of women at once?" he ventured.

"It seems to be a major talent you have." He could hear the smile in her voice.

"Only when I'm kissing you. You have the greatest lips in the world."

"Ooh, I like that," she crooned.

Harry could feel himself getting hard, and desperately tried to think of anything but Melissa. When he heard the office door open, and realized the guys had returned, he said, "I have to go now. The other deputies are back."

"Okay," Melissa said, but Harry could hear her pout.

"I'll see you tomorrow," he whispered, and hung up the phone.

He stood as the other two men sat down at their respective desks. "So how did the tour go?"

"It was fine," Dale said. "For a small town, you've got just about everything a guy could need."

"That's true. Is the town shutting up, Steve?"

"Yeah. We only have another hour on duty."

The phone rang once more and Harry answered it, wondering if it was Melissa again.

He was disappointed.

"It's Mike," the sheriff said in a low voice. "I need you and anyone else you can round up. We've got the rustlers pulling another raid."

"Give me your location," Harry stated. "And do we come in hard or soft?"

"Soft, unless you hear from me. You'll have your cell phone, won't you?"

"Yeah. We're on our way."

As soon as he got off the phone, he ordered Steve to call the closest deputy on night shift and get him in to answer the phones. Then Harry looked at Dale. "Do you want some action tonight? We've got cattle rustlers pulling a raid."

"Yeah, I want in, but I only have my hand pistol with me."

"No problem." Harry crossed the room and opened a locked gun case. He pulled out two shotguns and two 30-30 carbines.

Steve hung up the phone. "Fred will be here in five minutes."

"Let's roll," Harry called as he headed for the front door where the other SUV was parked. He handed Dale one of the shotguns and Steve one of the carbines, along with bullets. He kept the other two guns.

As they started off, Harry said, "The boss said to come in soft unless he notified us. When we get out of town, I'm turning off the lights and I'll need you to help me watch. I don't want to hit anything."

Within minutes, they came upon Mike's SUV, standing empty on the side of the road. Harry eased his vehicle to a stop behind it and quietly got out, urging the others to do the same.

They crept along the edge of the road until they

rounded a corner and saw a big 18-wheeler parked on the shoulder. They almost stepped on Mike.

Harry sank to the ground beside him. "There's three of us. Will that be enough, or do you want me to roust anyone out of bed?"

"That should be enough," Mike whispered. "We'll split up. I'll keep Steve with me. You and Wayne—" He stopped. "Who's here instead of Wayne?"

"Mike, meet Dale."

"Ah, welcome aboard, Dale. I hope Harry didn't force you to come with him."

"Nope, I volunteered," Dale whispered.

"Okay, Harry, you and Dale go to the other side of the 18-wheeler. Get an angle on the fence opening so you're not firing at us. Then, when they come into sight with the cattle, open fire."

"There's no one in the 18-wheeler?" Harry asked.

"I saw the driver get out and take one of the horses, and I haven't seen any movement since. But cross to the other side of the road and stay low."

"How about closing the fence?" Harry asked.

"You'd need some barbed wire and pliers. Do you have those?"

"Yeah, they're in the SUV. I'll go back and get them."

Harry left for a couple of minutes, and when he got back, motioned to Dale to follow him. They did as Mike had instructed, and after going past the 18-wheeler, Harry slipped to the fence and began repairing the gap. He felt his heart rate increasing, and hoped that trusting

Dale to warn him wouldn't be a mistake. After all, he didn't know him.

Harry didn't want to be caught off guard or get into trouble. His breathing became shallow at the thought of being shot tonight. He hadn't planned on not seeing Melissa again.

He worked quickly, hoping the repair job would hold. Dale called to him just as he was finishing up the last piece of fencing. Harry hurried back to his side.

"Did you see them?" he whispered, feeling the adrenaline rush again.

"No, but I heard cattle."

"Okay, we'll wait for Mike to open fire. When you shoot, aim high. We don't want any cattle or horses injured."

"Right."

The snow would make it easier to see, but it was still going to be difficult to hit their targets. But with the fence closed, the rustlers wouldn't have any place to go.

Suddenly, Mike fired. The deputies all joined in as the herd came into view. Harry worked to keep a steady aim. The rustlers were firing back, and a loud gun battle raged for a few minutes. Several of the horsemen galloped off across the ranch land. That left four. Two were down and the other two injured.

Mike asked him to undo the fence long enough to get the four horses and men through the opening. Harry approached each of the downed men carefully, holding his gun at the ready. No need. They were dead. He managed to get the two wounded men on their feet with Dale's help. Then they gathered the reins of the horses.

When they returned to the road the sheriff said, "You'll have to take the two wounded rustlers and Steve to the hospital."

Harry nodded. "You can keep Steve here if you need him," Harry said.

"No, I can't. He's wounded. I'll keep Dale."

"Is Steve hurt bad?" Harry asked, sympathy and concern immediately pouring through him. He'd been afraid that would happen to him.

"No. He's scared as much as anything. But we don't want to let him lose too much blood."

Harry handcuffed the two rustlers and got them into the back seat of the SUV. Then he put Steve, wounded in the arm, in the front with him. As he got started back to town, he called the hospital on his cell phone. "This is the Sheriff's Office. We're bringing in three wounded men. Two are cattle rustlers and the other is one of our deputies. Our ETA is five minutes."

He was pressing hard on the gas pedal. He didn't like the look of Steve, who was pale and sweaty. Steve might not be the best deputy, but he wanted to be; he worked hard and Harry had partnered with him for a long time.

Mentally he went over the encounter with the rustlers. Dale had certainly acquitted himself well. He'd followed orders without question and was willing to stay to help Mike with the details.

When Harry got to the hospital, both Jon and Caro

were there to meet them. To his surprise, Melissa came out after them.

"Melissa, what—"

She threw herself at him, cutting off any further words. Her arms went around his neck. "You weren't the one wounded? You're not hurt?" she demanded.

"No, Melissa," he said softly, taking a moment to hold her tightly against him. Then he had to put her aside. "I'm fine, honey, but I have to get these guys inside."

"Oh. Oh, yes. It was Steve who got wounded?"

"Yeah." He saw Caroline leading his partner into the clinic.

Jon was waiting to help him with the rustlers. Once they got them inside, Harry stayed in the room, his gun at the ready while they were evaluated and treated. Then he cuffed them to their beds in a standard precautionary procedure.

As he turned around, he almost ran over Melissa.

"Uh, honey, I've got to check on Steve."

Melissa, devouring him with her eyes, asked, "Will he be all right?"

"I don't know," Harry said, moving rapidly down the hall. Melissa followed him to the room where a nurse was working on the deputy.

Caroline entered right behind them. "Tell me what you found, Betsy."

"The bullet is still in his arm. He's lost a fair amount of blood and he's—" she lowered her voice "—scared out of his mind."

"All right." Caro stepped toward the wounded deputy. "Good evening, Steve. We're going to have to get that bullet out of you, but it won't be a problem. Do you want us to call your wife?"

"Yes, please. I want to see her before I go under."

Caroline glanced at Harry and he understood her unspoken request. He moved out into the hallway, accompanied by Melissa, and pulled out his cell phone. "Mrs. Lawson? This is Harry Gowan. I work with Steve. He's been injured— No, no, he's going to be fine. But they have to do a small operation to get a bullet out. He'd like for you to come down here before they operate."

Even Melissa could hear the hysterical woman crying into the phone.

"No, I can't come get you because I have to guard our prisoners," Harry said, and realized Melissa was tugging on his arm.

"I'll go get her. I'll borrow Caro's truck and go pick her up," she whispered.

Harry smiled at her in gratitude. "Yes, Melissa Randall is going to come get you. Just stay where you are and she'll be right there."

After hanging up the phone, he hugged Melissa and kissed her forehead. "Thanks, honey, I owe you one. The lady is hysterical. I should've expected it. I think Steve is, too."

"I'll hurry," Melissa promised. He gave her directions, and she went in the room to get the car keys from Caroline, who handed them over without question.

Harry thanked her for her cooperation, but the doctor just nodded. He could see she was putting all her efforts into soothing her patient. Steve was already hooked up to an IV drip, and he seemed calmer.

"I need to talk to Jon. Can you stay with Steve?" she asked.

"I'll go get him. The perps are cuffed and sedated."

"Thanks, Harry."

Fifteen minutes later Melissa was back. Harry knew it because he heard a hysterical woman enter the hospital. Steve's wife.

He had a feeling his partner wouldn't be on the force much longer. His wife had already wanted him to quit, and this injury would only make her more persistent. Besides, Steve would be more willing to consider leaving now.

Harry figured in a couple of weeks old Trev would be coming to Rawhide, just like he wanted.

At least it didn't appear Dale needed much training. Melissa slipped into the room.

"Thanks, honey, for going to get her. She would've had a wreck for sure if she'd driven herself."

"Yes, she almost made me have a wreck. She kept grabbing my arm, asking for reassurance. But no matter how often I tried to calm her, it didn't seem to help."

"Yeah. I don't think Steve will be long on the job."

"You think she'll make him resign?"

"I don't think it will take much pleading on her part,

Steve's not reacting much better than his wife. It's only a flesh wound!"

"Well, it's easy for us to say. We haven't been shot," Melissa muttered.

Harry gave a wry smile. "I have worse than Steve's. Ironically, it happened because he didn't do his job. He was a lot younger and greener then."

Melissa's eyes widened. "Where were you shot?"

"In the gut. But Caro said I got lucky. It missed my vital organs. I spent about a week in the hospital."

"Do you have a scar?" Melissa asked, her hands going to his chest, then sliding down his torso, as if feeling for the scar.

He stopped her before she let them slide too low. "Yeah, right about here, but you can't feel it through my clothes."

He'd dreamed of having her hands on him, albeit for different reasons. Now there was nothing sexual in her touch. Concern, not passion, was etched in her face.

Putting himself in the line of fire was part of his job, something he'd accepted long ago. He could tell from her expression Melissa wasn't used to it.

She looked at him, her big blue eyes serious. "I hadn't thought—"

She broke off then, but he knew what she was going to say. She hadn't thought about what could happen to him. For a moment there in the shootout, he had to admit he'd thought about dying and not seeing Melissa again.

He reached out and took her hand. "I know. But I'm

fine. Mike's fine, too. I assured Caroline of that as soon as I could. By the way, the new guy arrived this evening and went with us. I think he's going to be okay. He follows directions well."

Harry's phone rang, and with an apologetic look at Melissa, he answered it. It was the sheriff, giving him his orders for the night.

"No problem, Mike," he replied "I'll take care of them." Then Mike went on to fill him in about Dale Henry.

"I guess he's multitalented," Harry said a bit later. "Yeah, tell him to stop by here, and I'll give him the key to my apartment. Okay. Good night."

"Who's multitalented?" Melissa asked.

"The new deputy. He knows how to drive a big rig. He's bringing the truck into town tonight."

"But where will he park it?"

"In front of Mike's house for tonight."

Melissa frowned. "You know, they're my own family, but I don't even know where Mike and Caro live. Isn't that strange?"

"They have a cozy house on a back street close to the Sheriff's Office. But they're having another one built a little nearer the hospital."

"What are they going to do with their house when they move?"

"I guess sell it. I never asked Mike. Why?"

"I don't know. I just wondered."

"Well, you'd better get back to your mother. I'll be staying the night here with the prisoners."

"But that doesn't sound safe. What if you need help?"

With a grin, he said, "I'll push the call button."

THE SUN HAD JUST RISEN WHEN Melissa got up the next morning. She went immediately to the nurse's desk. "Have you talked to Harry this morning? Is everything all right?"

"It was at two, when I checked on the patients," the nurse, Betsy, said. Her eyes looked a little tired, Melissa noted.

"Maybe I should go check now."

"We were told not to let anyone in the room. It seems not all of the rustlers were captured last night."

Melissa's eyes widened. "Is it possible they might come here to see their friends?"

The nurse nodded. "According to the sheriff, that's a possibility. So far, though, no one has even called to ask about them."

"That's good. I suppose you'll order breakfast for them, too. You're busy. Do you want me to go to the café, and get the food for you? I don't mind."

"That would be great, Melissa. I'll call in the order and they'll pack it up and have it ready in fifteen minutes."

"I'll just go on down there and have some coffee while I wait."

Later, as Melissa was returning with the meals, she saw a pickup truck pull up in front of the hospital. It looked exactly like old man Lindstrom's rusty green truck, she decided. As teenagers, she and her friends had thought it would fall apart, but apparently it was still going.

Only it wasn't old man Lindstrom who got out.

Melissa immediately turned around and ran to the Sheriff's Office. She explained her fears to the deputies on duty, and one of them ran to the hospital, while the other called the nurse to warn Harry, then called the sheriff.

Melissa hoped she hadn't made a mistake, but she remembered Mr. Lindstrom had always left his key in the truck, figuring no one would steal it. But it appeared someone had.

Minutes later, when she reached the hospital with the food, she found all the excitement was over. The nurse told Melissa she'd spoken to Harry. He'd realized at once what was happening, pulled his gun, and hid by the door. He'd told the nurse to point the two men to their buddies room and then duck down behind the desk.

Harry had been holding the two visitors at gunpoint when two more deputies arrived. They'd put the rustlers in handcuffs and were leading them to the jail as Melissa walked in. Both thanked Melissa as she set the food down on the nurse's desk.

"Why did they thank you?" Harry asked her.

"Because I told them the robbers were here," she said, beaming at him.

"How did you know?"

"They pulled up in Mr. Lindstrom's truck. He always leaves the key in it. I figured they stole it. I was afraid I was wrong, but I thought I should tell them, anyway."

Harry hugged her right in front of the nurse and planted a quick but fervent kiss on her lips. "Good girl!"

"I wouldn't have thought of it, but Betsy told me two of the rustlers had escaped, and I know Mr. Lindstrom never lets anyone drive his truck."

Mike arrived just then, and Harry suggested he check on Mr. Lindstrom, relating Melissa's role in the successful capture of the two other rustlers.

"Good job, Melissa. You just saved us a lot of trouble. It would've been bad if we'd had a shootout here."

"Yes, it would have," Caroline proclaimed. She'd followed Mike in, determined to protect her hospital. She handed Mike a gun she was carrying. "You can take this back home. I'll just stay here."

"No you won't," he said, reaching for his wife. "You're going with me for breakfast." He kissed Caro and led her away, leaving Melissa with a smile on her face.

As MELISSA SHARED breakfast with her mother, she told her about her exciting morning.

"My goodness," Camille exclaimed. "That was very observant of you."

"Well, when I was a teenager my friends and I speculated about how much trouble we'd get in if we ever took his truck one night. We knew he always left the key in it. Then I thought about Dad and decided it wouldn't be worth it."

"Good. I'm glad. Mr. Lindstrom would be very upset. I guess he'll be upset now, too. Have they talked to him?"

"Harry said one of the deputies went out to his place

and checked on him," Melissa explained. "He was sleeping soundly."

Silence filled the room for a few minutes while they ate. Then Melissa said, "Mom, has Dad ever done something risky?"

"On a ranch, dear, most things are risky."

"I know, but—"

"You mean has he ever put himself in harm's way intentionally?"

"Yes."

"Once." She put down her fork and gave Melissa her complete attention. "Your cousin Jim went up into the mountains to save Patience and her little boy. The child's father had taken the boy away, intending to make him a soldier. I think he was three or four. Patience went after them because the sheriff at that time said he couldn't legally do anything.

"Jim went after her. When the other Randall men realized what he was facing, they formed a posse and followed his trail up into the mountains. Your father joined them."

"I had no idea!" Melissa exclaimed.

"So, to give you a short answer, yes, one time. And I couldn't disagree with your father for going. The Randalls have always stood together."

"Yes, that's one of the things I love about our family," Melissa said. "How does Caroline manage when Mike is in danger?"

"She struggles with it. But she knows he's really

good at what he does. And they seldom have injuries. Harry had a bad one, but it only happened because his partner wasn't well trained. That's when Mike started working hard on training and fitness."

"Yes, Harry was telling me, but I just hadn't realized... It finally hit me last night that he does dangerous work."

"But he's very good at what he does."

"Yes, I guess so."

"Caroline says she'd rather have whatever time she can spend with Mike than be with anyone else. I think all us Randall ladies feel the same way."

Melissa nodded, not saying anything, while thoughts of Harry filled her mind.

Chapter Ten

Harry and Dale were ready to set out for the Randall ranch the next morning to pick up some furniture when they stopped off at the Sheriff's Office to check in. "We're on our way, Mike," Harry announced.

He hadn't realized Mike was on the phone. The sheriff held up his hand for them to wait.

"That'll be fine. They're ready to go right now. Okay, I'll tell him."

He hung up the phone. "That was Melissa. She wants to ride out to the Randall ranch with the two of you."

"Sort of like taking a guide who understands the territory?" Harry teased, smiling.

Mike laughed. "More a case of her being on the bad side of the family. Apparently she hasn't visited yet."

Harry nodded. "Do we pick her up at the hospital?"

"Nope. She's coming down here." Mike turned to Dale. "Have you met Melissa yet?"

"Melissa who?" he asked.

"Melissa Randall," Harry clarified, though he didn't

want to. The last thing he wanted was for Dale and Melissa to get chummy.

"No, I haven't met her."

Harry whirled around as he heard rapid footsteps. Melissa hurried into the office. "I didn't hold you up, did I, Harry?"

"No, Melissa, you didn't hold us up. Uh, this is Dale Henry, our new deputy. Dale, this is Melissa Randall. She's only visiting. She's returning to Paris after the holidays."

"How do you do, Miss Randall," Dale said.

"Make it Melissa, please. There are way too many Randall women in town." She gave him a bright smile, but as hard as Harry studied the two of them, he didn't see any signs of flirtation.

"Are we ready to go?" he asked, starting toward the door.

"Yes," Melissa agreed, and Dale followed along behind them. When they reached the truck, they piled into the cab, Melissa in the center.

"Have you talked to Red and Mildred to see what furniture they have?" she asked.

"No," Harry answered, as he swung his truck onto the road. "I think Dale will pretty much take whatever they offer. He's not picky, right, Dale?"

"Absolutely. I'm grateful for the assistance," he said.

"Have you seen your apartment?" Melissa asked.

"No, Mike told me it was nice. That's good enough

for me. By the way, there are two apartments up there. Do you know who rents the other one?"

"I haven't heard," Harry said, not too interested in the topic.

Melissa and Dale talked occasionally on the drive out to the ranch, but Harry didn't say much. He didn't like Melissa spending this time with Dale, but he couldn't do anything about it.

When they reached the ranch, Melissa got out of the truck and began running toward the house.

Dale looked at Harry. "Why is she running?"

"She hasn't been to the ranch since she got home. Her mother had surgery on Sunday and she's been at the hospital with her."

"She's excited about seeing a couple of old people?"

Harry grabbed Dale's arm. "Listen and listen good. You show any disrespect to Mildred and Red and you will have made an enemy of every Randall in the county. And that means you'll be out of here before you can get settled."

"I didn't mean— I didn't understand."

"These two are the grandparents of the whole clan, even if they aren't kin to most of them. So treat them as if they were your grandparents—or pay a price."

"Okay, I've got it."

"Then come along and I'll introduce you."

When they reached the kitchen, they found Melissa surrounded by several of her aunts, as well as Red and

Mildred. Harry was warmly greeted, too. He introduced Dale.

"Welcome to Rawhide, young man." Red immediately filled two coffee mugs for them and offered them seats at the table, where a plate of cookies was waiting. "Help yourselves," he said, indicating the cookies. "You'd better hurry before the rest of them start eating."

"Red, we really appreciate what you're doing," Harry stated. "Dale was living in a furnished apartment in Cody, and he doesn't have anything but a television."

"Oh, good, 'cause we don't have a spare one of those," Red said.

Harry laughed, "I think a bed and maybe a sofa would be more important than a television, don't you, Dale?"

"Yeah. I'm getting too old to sleep on the floor."

"Anyone who can catch cattle rustlers deserves a good bed," a deep voice said. They all turned to see a tall, middle-aged man in the doorway.

Harry stood and extended his hand. "Hi, Jake. I didn't know you'd be here."

"We thought since you caught some cattle rustlers last night, maybe you deserved a little help today."

Dale stood in turn. "I'm Dale Henry, Mr. Randall. I appreciate your offer to help."

Jake shook his hand, too. "Welcome to Rawhide. I heard you did good work last night."

"I just did what Harry told me to do."

Jake smiled. "Harry's a good man. One of our favorites."

Melissa beamed at her uncle. "I think he's a good man, too."

"So I've heard, young lady," Jake said with a grin.

They were soon joined by Jake's three brothers, two of whom greeted their wives with a kiss. In short order they loaded three trucks with an assortment of furniture and volunteers.

When Harry turned to go, Mildred handed him a package of cookies. "Don't know why he's getting everything. Here's something you can snack on."

"Thanks, Mildred. You're the best," Harry said, and leaned over to kiss her cheek.

"Watch it, boy! She's my woman," Red teased.

Harry glanced ahead at Melissa and Dale. "I know exactly how you feel, Red."

"WHAT DO YOU HAVE THERE?" Melissa asked as Harry got into the truck with a box.

"Mildred gave me cookies as my reward."

"I'm glad you got something," she said, a hint of irritation in her voice.

"Hey, I'll share." Dale offered hastily. "Anything they're giving me you can have, Harry. I promise."

"No, thanks, Dale, but I appreciate the offer."

"I feel like such a fraud," the new deputy admitted. "Without you and Mike, I wouldn't have known what to do."

"Dale, just ignore Melissa. I hope that means she's on my side. That's more than enough of a reward," Harry said, giving her a warm smile.

She smiled back at him.

When they reached town again, Harry pulled into the parking lot behind Dale's apartment. "Come on, I'll introduce you to Russ Randall, your landlord," he said.

Melissa stayed to guard the truck while the men went into the accounting office to see Russ. In no time, her cousin came out to help them unload.

"Hi, Melissa," he said in greeting. "I didn't know I'd get to see you today."

"I rode out to the ranch with them so I could say hello to Red and Mildred. They were complaining, you know."

Russ laughed. "Yeah, I know." Then he noticed the other two trucks pulling up, and his parents in front. "Dad? Mom? I didn't know you were both coming." He turned to look at Dale. "I didn't know you'd get such a welcome."

Pete came over to greet his son. "Well, we're happy to help Dale, but we also came to have enchiladas for lunch. It is enchilada day, isn't it?"

Russ laughed. "Yes, it is, and I might just have to join you. I'll call my wife and let her know."

As he took out his cell phone, everyone grabbed something and began climbing the stairs. With all the willing workers, the furniture was unloaded and put in place in no time. Then Melissa joined two of her aunts, Janie and Anna, on a shopping trip.

"I'm glad you're all helping Dale," Melissa said to her aunts, "but Mike and Harry did most of the work last night with those rustlers. Harry even caught the other two rustlers this morning."

Anna patted her shoulder. "We know, honey, but they're going to be rewarded monetarily. They don't need all this stuff."

"Oh. Is that a secret?"

"I think so. I just wanted you to know that we're not forgetting them. And Steve will get something, too. I'm not sure what."

"Thanks for telling me, Aunt Anna."

Aunt Janie grinned at her. "We know you're just standing up for your man."

"No," she stuttered. "I mean, he's not-- We're just friends."

"Yeah, we heard," Janie said with a laugh. "You go, girl!"

Melissa turned bright red and didn't say anything else. Instead she focused on purchasing linens and kitchenware for the new deputy. Debating over what comforter to pick was a safer topic.

By now, Dale's apartment was completely functional. He was quite stunned by the nice apartment and furnishings, and all the work donated by the Randalls.

"All right, it's lunchtime. I'm buying. Let's go," Jake called to everyone.

"I think I should buy lunch for all of you," Dale suggested.

"No, boy, you can buy after you've been here a few years."

Melissa made sure she sat next to Harry at lunch. It wasn't hard to do, since all the family expected it. And they made sure Dale was at the other end of the table.

Melissa didn't care where Dale sat as long as she was sitting next to Harry. She was so glad her family hadn't forgotten his role in apprehending the bad guys. The sheriff's department had completely destroyed the ring of rustlers.

"Did Mike commend you for your work last night and this morning?" Melissa asked him.

Harry turned to stare at her. "Why would he?"

"Well, you were part of the raid last night. You guarded the other two men all night long and then caught the last two."

"But I might not have caught the last two if you hadn't noticed Mr. Lindstrom's truck."

"No, you would've caught them anyway. I know."

"Honey, you might be a little prejudiced, which I'm pleased about. But Mike doesn't sit around singing our praises because we do our job."

Melissa stuck her nose in the air. "Well, I think he should. You could've been shot!"

"You mean like Steve?"

She nodded.

"That's not going to happen." Harry said in a soothing voice. "I take time to properly assess a situation, and use caution."

Melissa looked up at him. "I hope you always do," she said softly.

Harry leaned forward, and Melissa thought he was going to kiss her right there. But the waitress arrived with their food, and he turned away.

Melissa sighed. She wanted him to kiss her. It seemed to be all she could think about.

Her mother! Melissa remembered then that she hadn't told her she'd be gone for lunch. She excused herself from the table and walked outside, pulling out her cell phone.

"Mom? It's Melissa. I didn't think I'd be gone this long, but Uncle Jake took us all to the café and—"

She broke off as a strong arm slid around her waist. She looked up to see Harry frowning at her, a questioning look on his face.

"Are you okay?" he whispered.

She nodded. "Yeah, Mom, I'm sorry. Oh, you do? Okay, thanks. I'll see you in a little while."

She hung up the phone and leaned into Harry's embrace. The warmth of his arms heated her immediately. Looking into his chocolate-brown eyes, she whispered, "Should I say I'm going back to Paris?"

He smiled. "Honey, I can't kiss you out on the street. We made that mistake once."

"Just a little kiss?"

He bent over her and pecked her lips with his. "Maybe…you can come up to my apartment after lunch and I can really kiss you."

"You don't have to go to work?"

"Yeah, but I can take a minute or two. If I don't get a real kiss soon, I may go into withdrawal. You wouldn't want that, would you?"

"Definitely not!" Melissa exclaimed, and reached up to give him a brief kiss as down payment.

"Okay, let's go finish our lunch."

She wanted to tell him she didn't care about lunch, but Harry was a big man. He probably needed his food. So she returned to the restaurant with him, completely oblivious to the stares of everyone in the café, including a large number of Randalls.

She could barely eat, thinking about going upstairs to Harry's apartment.

"Are you okay?" her aunt Janie whispered.

"Oh, yes! I went out to call Mom. I hadn't told her I'd be gone so long. But she's had lunch and is feeling fine. She told me to take my time."

"Oh, good. Anna and I are going to visit her before we head back to the ranch."

"I'll probably see you there, but…I've got a few errands to run first." Her one and only errand was kissing Harry Gowan.

"No problem. We'll keep her company."

"Thanks. She'll enjoy that."

Melissa finished her lunch quickly, but continued to chat with those around her, keeping an eye on Harry's progress. When everyone stood to go, she breathed a sigh of relief and felt her heartbeat speed up. She was going to be alone with Harry, where no one could interrupt them, even for five minutes.

She could feel her cheeks heating up, and hoped everyone would think it was exposure to the cold air. When Harry reached down and surreptitiously clasped her hand, she held on to his as if it was her anchor.

When they reached the sidewalk, everyone split up.

Harry turned toward the Sheriff's Office. Melissa moved with him, anticipating her time alone with him.

Dale called out to Harry, "I'll be right over, as soon as I change."

Harry nodded. "I'll see you there." But he passed by the door to the Sheriff's Office and headed for the stairs leading up to his apartment. He looked down at her. "Okay?"

"Oh, yes," she said, smiling brilliantly.

They started up the stairs, only to be stopped by a booming voice.

It belonged to her father.

Chapter Eleven

"Hey, Harry and Melissa, where are you going?" Griff called as he walked toward them up the street.

Harry wondered if his guilty conscience had sent out a signal to Melissa's dad. A kind of beacon that illuminated a couple headed to a romantic rendezvous.

"I—I was going to show Melissa my apartment," he said. "She wanted to see it after touring Dale's new place." He figured that was as good a reason as any.

"Oh, good, I'll come, too. I haven't seen it since the repairs."

Harry met Melissa's tortured glance and looked away. At least he knew it wasn't her happiest moment, either.

"Sure. Though, actually, it's not that interesting. But at least it's fairly clean today, because Dale slept here last night."

Slowly, so Griff wouldn't notice, he removed his hand from Melissa's and led the way up the stairs. He unlocked the door and then stood back until both Randalls had entered.

Griff looked around, assessing the place with a keen eye. "They fixed it up real nice," he said. "No bullet holes in sight."

"There were bullet holes?" Melissa asked. She looked at Harry, fear and concern in her eyes.

"Yeah, there were a few." He walked into the kitchen area. "Anybody want a drink?"

"No thanks," she murmured. "Who did the shooting?"

Griff offered the explanation. "Steve was working undercover in L.A."

Melissa stopped him right away. "You mean the deputy? He worked for the FBI?"

"No. Your cousin Jessica's husband, Steve, though, of course, they weren't married then. Anyway, Jessica had finished with her movie and decided to come home. She found Steve in her alley. He talked her into not calling the cops, and she put him in her car and brought him home. He'd discovered his partners and his boss in Washington were dirty. They came after him."

"So he shot them here?"

"Not exactly," Griff said. "You see, Jessica was staying here with Steve. One of the guys got past Mike and broke in. It was Jessica who killed him."

Melissa stared at her father, her mouth agape, then turned to Harry. "I can't believe it." She shook her head. "I don't know that I could've been that strong."

"You don't need to be. That was an extraordinary situation." Harry moved nearer to her again, more than anything he wanted to pull her close to him, to let her draw from his strength. It was killing him not to take her in his arms. But he couldn't.

Then, to make matters worse, Griff suggested, "Let's look at the bedroom." Without waiting, he went into the room.

Harry took full advantage of being alone for a moment, and pulled Melissa to him for a quick kiss. But it only whetted his appetite for more. Then he walked with her into the bedroom.

"Hey, you've got a great view of the town," Griff remarked.

"Yeah. That's one of the good things about this apartment."

"For a policeman," Griff said. "I mean, most people would rather have a view of the Rockies."

Harry shrugged. "To each his own."

The older man nodded. "Well, thanks for the tour. They did a great job with the repairs. We've got to get to the hospital. Ready, Melissa?"

She looked her father in the eye. "I'll be right there, Dad, as soon as I have a moment with Harry."

"One moment? I'll wait," Griff agreed with a smile.

"No, Dad. One moment *alone*."

Father and daughter stared at each other for several seconds.

Finally, Griff nodded. "I'll wait downstairs."

As soon as he left the apartment, Melissa threw herself into Harry's arms. He didn't hesitate to kiss her, not needing his convenient excuse of kissing her goodbye.

He claimed her with purpose, his tongue entering her mouth to engage hers in a frenzied dance. Never before had he kissed a woman with this much pent-up desire, and he made sure his lips conveyed all that emotion.

Neither he nor Melissa broke the kiss; it was all they'd have, until they heard Griff bellow up from downstairs. "Melissa!"

Reluctantly pulling away, Harry muttered a curse.

She rested her head on his chest and let out a deep sigh. "I have to go."

"I know. Me, too."

"So I guess you kissed me goodbye again, huh?"

"I guess so."

But as he watched her walk out the door, he realized the goodbye game was no longer one he wanted to play. His arms felt empty without her.

"YOU MADE ME FEEL LIKE a schoolgirl, Dad, and I'm not!" Melissa lambasted her father even as they walked down the street.

"You were going to a man's apartment in the middle of the day, when everyone could see you! You need to consider your family's reputation around here!"

"You, of course, have never done anything like that, have you? Isn't that what Mom was telling me yesterday? That she was a month pregnant when you got married?"

"Are you planning on getting married soon? 'Cause if you are, I haven't heard about it!" Griff retorted, walking even faster.

Melissa sped up to stay even with her father. "Had you asked Mom to marry you when you slept with her? Tell me, Dad, and remember I'm going to ask Mom that question when we get to the hospital."

"That's different, and you know it! You're planning on going back to France. You're just making out with Harry and then you're going to dump him!"

"Oh, so you can read the future? Can you tell me what's happening tomorrow, or next week, or is it only my behavior you can determine in advance?"

"Tell me you're staying here and I'll escort you back to Harry's apartment myself. But if you can't tell me that, then I have nothing to say to you except behave yourself."

"I'm not a child!" Melissa screamed at him.

"Then quit acting like one!"

They came to an abrupt halt as they entered the waiting room of the hospital and came face-to-face with the four Randall brothers.

"Afternoon, Griff, Melissa. How are you two doing?" Jake asked, his gaze alternating between the two of them.

"Uh, we're fine. Have you been in to see Camille?" Griff inquired, trying to pretend nothing was wrong.

But Melissa stepped forward. "We're not fine, Uncle Jake. Dad keeps treating me like I'm a child!"

Her uncle Brett leaned forward. "Now, Melissa, it's hard for a dad to let a daughter grow up."

"You let Jessica go to Hollywood!" Melissa retorted.

"So? I let you go to France!" Griff pointed out.

"You only did so because Mom wouldn't speak to you until you agreed!" Melissa turned and almost spat the words at her father.

"Fine! At least I did agree! And now you have to come back to my hometown and ruin your family's reputation?"

As Melissa opened her mouth to respond, her aunt Anna stepped into the room. "Camille wants to see Melissa and Griff now."

They both paled, and Griff looked at his daughter. "We shouldn't have been yelling."

"I know that. But—but you provoked me!"

"Camille is waiting." Anna held the door open.

Like children called to the principal's office, they walked slowly down the hall.

Aunt Janie was with the patient, but she excused herself as they came in.

Camille was sitting up in bed, looking very alert. "You both are certainly in good voice this afternoon," she said softly.

Griff went to her bedside. "Honey, I lost my temper. I'm sorry."

Melissa hung her head. "Me, too."

"You two are so much alike," Camille said with a sigh.

"No, we're not!" Griff exclaimed.

Melissa kept her head down. "I know."

He whirled around to stare at her. "No, we're not!"

Camille shook her head. "Dear, it's true. At least Melissa realizes it."

"Oh, sure, and next you'll tell me she's right."

"About what?" Camille asked, looking directly at her husband.

"She was— Well, it was— Nothing. Never mind. It doesn't matter."

"Then why were you yelling in the waiting room?"

"Not just the waiting room, Mom," Melissa told her. "All the way down the street from the Sheriff's Office to the hospital."

Camille covered her eyes with her hand.

"Honey, probably no one noticed!" Griff told her.

She dropped her hand and stared at him. "Are you out of your mind? You yelled out on the main street of Rawhide and you think no one noticed? What were you yelling about?"

"She was going upstairs to Harry's apartment, just the two of them!"

"And?"

"I couldn't let her do that, so I went up with them. And when I said we had to get to the hospital, she asked for a moment alone with Harry. I went downstairs and waited almost five minutes. Then I yelled up for her to come down. When she got there, she told me I made her feel like a schoolgirl!"

"Amazing," Camille said. "It's a good thing I'm getting out of the hospital today, before the two of you decide to have a discussion about the birds and the bees in the middle of the street, too. They could sell tickets to that one."

"You get to go home today?" Melissa asked in surprise. "Now? You can go home now?"

"Yes, if anyone will volunteer to take me there."

Griff finally recognized a cue he knew. "I'll volunteer," he said at once.

"We both will, Mom," Melissa assured her. "I'll pack your bag."

MELISSA QUICKLY CHANGED the sheets on her parents' bed and piled up the pillows for her mother. Griff wanted to carry her in, but Camille insisted on walking.

"The nurse said I should keep on my feet. It's the best thing for me." She sat on the edge of the bed. "I'm not sure I should lie down yet. It's early in the afternoon."

"The nurse also said you should take a nap when you got home, remember?" Melissa pointed out.

"Okay, but don't fuss over dinner, dear."

"I won't, Mom. I'll take care of everything," Melissa promised. She wished she could invite Harry for dinner, but he worked late hours.

"Do you want me to stay with you, honey?" Griff asked.

"No, you'd better go tend the cows while I'm napping."

"And, Dad?" Melissa called before he could leave the room. Her father stopped and looked at her. "I think you need to tell John what a good job he's doing. He's very worried about pleasing you."

Griff stared at her. "You're kidding."

"No, when Harry was here after we moved the

herd, he told me John was afraid he'd mess something up now that you've turned the ranching over to him. I just thought—"

"Yeah. I'll tell him," Griff said gruffly, and hurried out the door.

"John never mentioned that he felt inadequate about taking over," her mother said.

"No one wants to confess their weaknesses to you, Mom. You're so sweet to everyone."

"You'd think they might trust me to help."

"You can't do everything, Mom. Now, tell me what you want for dinner."

By the time they'd discussed the options, Camille was ready for her nap. Melissa left the room with a sigh. It was good to have her mother back home again.

When she got to the kitchen, she picked up the phone and called the Sheriff's Office. Dale answered.

"Is Harry there?" she asked.

"No, ma'am, he's out on a call. Can someone else help you?"

"It's Melissa. Will you tell him I'm back at the ranch and to please call me here when he gets in?"

"Sure will, Melissa."

She got started on dinner, hoping Harry would phone. The longer she went without hearing from him, the more her imagination had him in desperate struggles, maybe even gun battles.

Finally, around five o'clock, she called the Sheriff's Office again. Harry answered the phone.

"Why didn't you phone me? I've been imagining all kinds of terrible things," she told him at once.

"Melissa? Aren't you at the hospital?"

"No. I guess Dale didn't tell you I called," she said, taking a deep breath.

"Just a minute," Harry said. He must have covered the receiver with his hand, but she could still hear him talking to Dale.

"Oh, yeah," the new deputy replied "I'm sorry I forgot to tell you."

"Write messages down next time, okay? There's a notepad on your desk."

Then Harry came back to her. "Sorry, honey. Dale forgot to tell me."

"When I phoned, he said you were out on a call. Was it dangerous?"

"No. It was a ten-year-old shoplifting at the general store."

"Oh. I was afraid you'd been in another gun battle."

"Honey, they don't happen that often around here. I go months without even drawing my weapon, much less firing it."

"I know, but— Well, I called to let you know that we brought Mom home today. So I won't be hanging out at the hospital anymore."

"Too bad. I was hoping to see you at dinner when I went to the café to get our orders."

"I wish I could be there. But I'm fixing dinner here. Oh, Harry, can you join us on Sunday? Mom won't be well enough to go to dinner at the main ranch, so it would be nice to have a guest here."

"Sure, I'll be glad to volunteer."

"You don't have to work on Sunday, do you?"

"No, I'm off all day."

"Good. Come at noon, or after church, whichever works for you. Mom and I will be here, even if Dad and John go to church."

"All right, I'll see you on Sunday."

"And—and you could phone me if you want to. Sometime when you're not busy."

"Okay, Melissa. I'll do that."

"Stay safe," she whispered, and then said goodbye. She didn't want to hang up the phone, but she had chores to complete.

She'd tell her parents tonight that she'd invited Harry to Sunday dinner. Hopefully, neither of them would object.

AS DALE AND HARRY ATE dinner—just the two of them, since Steve was still out on sick leave—Dale said, "Hey, did I tell you I found out who lives in the other apartment?"

Harry didn't much care as long as it wasn't Melissa, but he asked, "Who?"

"Two nurses. They're both really cute, but there's one named Betsy. I really liked her."

"Oh, yeah, she was at the hospital yesterday when the rustlers came in. She seemed like a good nurse."

"Man, I don't care about that. She has a great body and the prettiest face."

"Remember, you represent the Sheriff's Office, either on duty or off, so don't do anything that would reflect badly on us."

"You take things a bit too seriously, don't you, Harry?" Dale asked with a big grin.

"I don't think so," he muttered, and took another bite of his hamburger. He would prefer not to have this conversation with Dale right now.

"Say, where do you and Melissa go to have fun around here?"

"Melissa and I aren't dating, Dale. And the only place I know of is the steak house with the bar in it. It's busy on the weekend."

"What do you mean, you and Melissa aren't dating?" Dale asked in surprise.

"It's a long story, but it doesn't matter, because she's going back to France."

Just saying those words evoked a vision of Melissa—her short hair, dark brown like most of the Randalls, those amazing blue eyes, and most of all, those incredible lips.

Harry stood up suddenly. "I'm going to walk the town."

Before he could move, however, the door opened and a stranger entered. "*Excusez-moi*. I am looking for a Randall."

It didn't take a genius to realize the stranger was French. Or to immediately associate him with Melissa. After all, Rawhide didn't have many foreign visitors.

With his heart sinking, Harry stepped forward. "Which Randall are you looking for?" As if there was any doubt!

"That is not your business!" the man exclaimed, his nose in the air. "Just tell me where."

"I only asked because we have a lot of Randalls. There's Jake, Pete, Brett, Chad, Josh, Rich, Russ, Toby, John, Jim…" Harry intentionally named only the men in the large family.

"Melissa Randall," the stranger snapped, glaring at him.

"Melissa? Are you sure?"

"*Oui,* I am sure. She is my fiancée."

In spite of the man's accent, Harry understood his words, and his heart sank like a stone.

Had Melissa been playing a game with him? Not only was she going back to France, but she was also going to marry a Frenchman! She'd had no right…. Of course, he hadn't asked her if she was involved with anyone before he'd kissed her.

Harry didn't like that thought. He wanted to be angry with Melissa. Something he was doing a good job of without attaching any blame to himself.

Abruptly, he said, "I'll take you. Come on."

"I have my own car. I will follow you."

"Yeah, you do that," Harry muttered. "Dale, I'll be back in a few minutes."

He strode out of the office to the SUV parked in front. The stranger followed him. It occurred to Harry that he hadn't asked the man his name. But what did it matter? "Melissa's fiancé" was sufficient.

All the way out to Griff's place, he muttered under his breath, trying to think what to say to Melissa that would convey his disdain for her behavior. He wanted to sound cool and amused, but all the words he came up with were angry and hot.

"How dare you" wasn't a good way to sound uninvolved. "What the hell were you doing, kissing me when you were already engaged?" definitely wouldn't sound unfazed. Harry took a deep breath and unclenched his teeth as he pulled into the driveway of the Haney ranch. He checked for headlights in his rearview mirror, finally remembering the man following him.

He was still there.

Harry parked the SUV and was knocking at the door before the man had even parked his car.

Melissa swung open the door, first surprise and then pleasure appearing on her face.

He'd take care of that, Harry thought with almost grisly satisfaction.

"Harry, I didn't expect you. I'm so glad you dropped by. Did you get off work early?"

"No. I'm here in an official capacity," he practically growled. Her father reached the door by that time, but Harry ignored him. "I've brought you something you apparently lost."

"What?"

"Your *fiancé!*" he roared, stepping aside.

"*Ma chérie,* I have missed you so!" the Frenchman said with enthusiasm, his arms extended to Melissa.

Even Harry, blinded by jealousy, noticed that she stepped backward, not forward.

"Your *what?*" Griff demanded.

"No! No, he's not," Melissa protested, still trying to back up, though her father was in her way.

"*Mais oui,* Melissa, you know it is true!"

"Go away, Pierre! I don't want you here!"

"Are you telling the truth, Melissa?" Harry demanded at the same time.

Camille appeared behind Griff. "Why doesn't everyone come in? It's too cold to keep the door open. Oh, you must be Pierre. Were we expecting you?"

Harry almost snorted aloud. As if visitors from Paris dropped by every day!

"*Non,* it is a surprise for Melissa," Pierre replied with a brilliant smile.

Judging by the stunned look in Melissa's eyes, Harry thought, his arrival was more than a surprise. It was a shock.

MELISSA WANTED TO RUN AND hide. She certainly didn't want to respond to Pierre's outstretched arms Nor did she want to face the anger in Harry's eyes. But she was no longer a child. She had to deal with the mess. Even if it wasn't her fault.

They entered the family room and Melissa immediately chose a single chair, making it impossible for Pierre to get close to her.

The others took seats, too, at her mother's invitation. Griff was the first to speak. "Melissa, is it true you're engaged to this man?"

"No, it's not, Dad," she said hurriedly.

"But it is, Melissa. You know we made plans!" Pierre exclaimed.

"No! I mean, yes! But I canceled them!" She took a quick peek at Harry, but couldn't bear his angry expression.

"You mean you *were* engaged to him?" her father demanded. "You never told us that!"

"I—I was going to tell you after I got here, but we broke off our engagement before I left Paris. And you know that, Pierre, so don't play dumb!"

"What is this 'play dumb'?" he asked.

"Acting like you don't know what she's talking about," Harry explained helpfully.

"But, *chérie,* I do not want to end our agreement. I am here to win your heart."

"No!" Melissa protested. She didn't leave any room for hope in her response, but she knew Pierre was always sure he was right. About everything.

Pierre turned to her mother, "She is angry, but she does not mean what she says."

John, who had been peacefully watching television before the room had been invaded, said, "Are we talking about the same Melissa?"

His sister glared at him, then thought better of her reaction. Maybe he could help her convince Pierre of her stubbornness. "You'd better listen to him, Pierre. I can be very difficult."

"I do not even know this person. Why should I listen to him?"

"He's my brother. He's known me all my life."

Camille stepped in. "Pierre, this is my son, John. John, this is your sister's…friend from Paris."

"Her fiancé," Pierre corrected firmly. "Pierre de Leon."

"Stop saying that! I'm not your fiancée," Melissa said. She wasn't sure how she would convince Pierre, but she was determined she would. She wanted him out of Rawhide.

"You must give me a chance to explain, *ma chère.* You asked too much of me. It is unreasonable of you to think I must remain faithful to you all my life. A man has needs." He added that brilliant smile again, as if he thought it would convince her.

"Welcome to the twenty-first century, Pierre. American women don't buy such trash!" Melissa responded.

Pierre looked at her father. "Tell her, *monsieur.* I am sure you understand what I have said."

Griff, red-faced, immediately exclaimed, "Are you telling me that you cheated on my daughter?"

Pierre shrugged his shoulders. "Of course. A man must have several lovers. That does not mean he does not love his wife or take care of her." Again he gazed at each male in the room, as if for confirmation.

Griff stood. "I agree with my daughter. You need to leave our home. My daughter will not marry someone like you."

Pierre stood to face him. "My family is descended from royalty. She would be a fool to reject me. It is enough that I have come all this way."

"No, it's not!" Melissa spoke for herself. "Just go!"

"Where do I go? My flight does not leave until Sunday afternoon. I thought I would spend time here and make a better acquaintance with your parents."

"Go back to Buffalo and find a hotel." Melissa, as well as the rest of the people in the room, knew there was no hotel in Rawhide.

"No. I must stay here to convince you, *ma chère.*" With that, he sat back down.

Camille broke the stunned silence. "I'm sorry, Pierre, but I think it's best you don't stay here."

"I think I know where he can stay," Harry interjected.

"Where?" Griff barked.

"Dale has a second bedroom in the apartment. I'm sure he'd take Pierre in for three nights."

"Who is this Dale and where does he live?" Pierre demanded testily.

"He's another deputy in the Sheriff's Office. He was there when you came in, and his apartment is just across the street."

Pierre gave an autocratic nod. "I accept."

"I'll have to call Dale and get his okay." Harry looked at Camille for permission to use the phone.

She nodded and rose to escort him to the phone in the kitchen. She whispered, "Thank you, Harry."

"No problem. I'm sure Dale will agree."

A couple of minutes later he returned to a tense silence. "Dale says he'll be glad to let you stay, Pierre. He owes the Randalls a lot and is happy to do anything for them."

"Fine." Melissa said, standing. "Now you have a place to stay. And be sure you don't miss your plane on Sunday!"

"Where will I eat? I do not cook for myself!" Pierre said.

Harry had the answer. "The café is across the street from your apartment. You can take all your meals there."

"Ah, *bon*. And you will join me for lunch tomorrow, Melissa?"

"No!" she said, amazed, once again, by his audacity, "I'm not accompanying you anywhere."

"Dear," Camille said softly.

"But, Mom—"

"I'm not saying I want you to marry this man. I don't. But he is alone in a strange place. I think you should accompany him to lunch tomorrow."

Melissa gave in to her mother's wishes. "Fine. Not that it'll do him any good." And with that, she stalked out of the family room.

By the time she made it to her bedroom, the tears she'd held back were flowing freely. Swiping at them, she threw herself on her bed. Why did Pierre have to follow her—to Rawhide, of all places? Everyone in town would know the story in about half an hour.

But the most important person had actually witnessed the scene. Harry.

She'd never forget the look on his face when he'd said, "Your fiancé."

Becoming engaged to Pierre had been a colossal mistake, she knew now. He'd swept her off her feet about a year ago when they'd met at a sidewalk café on the Left Bank, where she'd gone to do some sketches. Suave and worldly, he'd wowed her and wooed her, until she couldn't resist dating him, being with him, and finally accepting his proposal.

She'd overlooked a lot, how he hadn't approved of her apartment, her friends. How he'd tried to blind her to his faults—numerous as they were—by impressing her with his family's wealth and position. But in the end, nothing about Pierre de Leon had impressed her—not when she'd seen him with another woman.

She'd taken his ring off her hand and thrown it at him, and she stalked out, she'd told him the engagement was off and she never wanted to see him again.

Why hadn't that convinced him?

And more importantly, she thought now, through her tears, how was she going to convince Harry?

Chapter Twelve

Despite having little sleep, Harry came in to work early to get his workout over for the day. He intended to be standing outside to watch Melissa meet Pierre. Harry wanted to be sure she didn't join him in his apartment. Though what he would do if she did, he didn't know.

He gritted his teeth. If she did that, he'd never kiss her again. Or talk to her, for that matter.

He shrugged off the other deputies' questions about why he was in so early. In the weight room he tried to do too much, a kind of macho response that he didn't want to think about. After he finished his workout, he showered and dressed and entered the Sheriff's Office.

"Hey, Harry, here's a message for you," one of the day guys called out.

Harry took the slip of paper and stared at it. He hadn't expected a call from Melissa. Was she phoning to tell him she was going back to France with Pierre?

He dialed the number with foreboding. When Camille answered, he said, "Melissa left a message for me to call."

"Yes, I know, Harry. She left already, but she wanted you to go to lunch with her and Pierre. And I want you to go, too. I don't trust that man!"

"Me, neither, but I can't talk Melissa out of anything. She has to make her own decision."

"Of course, I agree. But I'd feel better if you go with her. Could you?"

"Yeah, I could go for an hour. But are you sure that's a good idea?"

"Yes, I do. Thank you very much."

"Okay. Will she come here before she goes to the café, or should I meet her there?"

"She said she'd head to your office."

"Okay, Camille. Thanks."

After he hung up the phone, he stepped into Mike's office to go over some business. The sheriff was curious about the Frenchman, but Harry didn't say much about him.

"I may drop by the café to meet him," Mike mused. "I could try out my French."

"Sure, why not?" Harry said, his voice tight. He stepped outside the office to wait for Melissa. He didn't want to discuss anything in front of his coworkers.

Five minutes later, she pulled into a parking space close to the office, got out of the car and approached him. "Did you talk to Mom?"

"Yes." He wasn't going to make it easy for her.

"Will you go to lunch with me and Pierre?"

"I told your mother I would, but I have some conditions."

"What are they?"

"You sit beside me, not Pierre. You don't go anywhere with him no matter what he says. And at the end of an hour, I have to be at work again, so you go home. Not with Pierre."

"I don't *want* to go anywhere with him!" she exclaimed, her voice full of anger.

"Do you agree to those terms?" Harry asked, not easing his stance.

"Yes, of course."

"Good. Then let's go."

He didn't touch her during their short walk. They both saw Pierre come out of Dale's apartment and wave to Melissa. When they reached the door to the café, they stood beside it, waiting as he crossed the street.

"Bonjour, ma chère," he said, putting his hands on her shoulders and bending down to kiss her.

Melissa jerked out of his hold. "Harry is coming to lunch with us."

Pierre turned to stare at him. "You are not on duty?" he asked, looking at his uniform shirt.

"No." Harry put his hand on Melissa's back to guide her into the restaurant.

Pierre frowned. "You are a friend of Melissa? You have known her many years?"

Harry didn't want to answer that second question. "Long enough," he replied.

Pierre stared at him, not clear about what he'd said. Then the Frenchman realized he was being left behind, and hurried after them. When he reached the booth they had chosen, he found Melissa sitting against the wall and Harry firmly in place beside her.

"Have a seat, Pierre," Harry said calmly, indicating the bench across from him and Melissa.

"But it is right that *I* sit with Melissa. She is my fiancée."

Harry shook his head and clucked his tongue. "We have an expression in the United States, Pierre. 'Wake up and smell the coffee.'" Seeing his confused expression, Harry made his meaning clear. "Melissa broke off your engagement." With a snap, he opened his menu. "Now, I can recommend the enchiladas."

Pierre stood there, sputtering. Then, as if instructed to compose himself, he took a breath and puffed out his chest. "What are enchiladas?" he asked.

Harry gave him a detailed explanation until the waitress came to take their drink orders.

"I have not seen your wine list," Pierre said, finally sitting down.

Beatrice put her hand on her ample hip. "Honey, don't get cute with me. I've got other customers."

Harry smiled at Beatrice, who'd been working at the café for decades. "I'll take care of this." He turned to Pierre. "This is small-town Wyoming, not France," he said. "Wine is not served at everyday restaurants. Here you drink beer, iced tea or water. So which would you like?"

Pierre looked outraged. "I will have water."

Beatrice wrote that down, along with Harry and Melissa's orders.

But when she brought Pierre a glass of water, he blustered, "What is this? Where is the bottle?"

"It's water, honey." Beatrice had lost her patience. "Take it or leave it."

He shooed her away with his hand, then looked at Melissa. "She is rude."

Melissa laughed, and Harry had to struggle not to join her. He was having too much fun trying to get Pierre's goat.

He asked how Pierre knew English so well.

"I studied at Oxford for four years."

It figured he'd go to a fancy school. No ordinary one for Pierre. For some reason, that annoyed Harry. But annoyance was quickly replaced by amusement again when Beatrice brought Pierre his enchiladas. The man didn't know what to make of his food, while Harry and Melissa dug right in.

When they finished, Harry got up to go to work, Melissa following him out of the booth.

"Goodbye, Pierre," she said coolly. "Have a nice trip back."

"But we will visit now that the officer must return to work."

"No, we will not." Melissa started out of the café.

"*Non!*" Pierre yelled, and stood to grab her arm.

"Take your hands off her!" Harry ordered, advancing on him.

"Is there a problem here, Harry?" a deep voice asked.

He turned to find his boss no more than fifteen feet away.

"No, I—" he began, but Mike interrupted him. The sheriff walked up to Pierre and rattled off something in French. Whatever he said made the man's face heat up.

Harry leaned in to Melissa. "What's he saying?"

"Trust me, you don't want to know." She took hold of his arm and started walking. "Lets get out of here."

"IS SOMETHING ON YOUR mind?" Camille asked Melissa the next morning, catching her by surprise.

"I—I've been thinking about Harry." She felt her cheeks flush, just saying his name.

"He's a wonderful man. I'm surprised some woman hasn't snatched him up by now."

"Well, it won't be Betsy. I've steered Dale in her direction."

"Why did you do that?" Camille asked calmly.

"To— Uh, because I thought they made a good couple." Melissa had been about to say because she wasn't going to let the nurse get hold of Harry, but that was a little too much honesty to share.

"Well, there are other women," Camille said before she took a sip of her coffee.

Her mother could always read her, Melissa mused.

"I know," she said glumly, propping her chin in her hand. "Out of sight, out of mind."

"Yes, too bad you're going back to France."

"I'm not staying in France, Mom."

Camille stared at her daughter. "You're not? When did you make this decision?"

"It's been evolving slowly." In truth, she'd been debating it even before she'd left Paris, but she'd made the decision a few days ago. Yesterday's fiasco with Pierre had sealed the deal. "Don't say anything to Dad yet. I won't be staying in Rawhide, either. I want to start my own company and I'm thinking New York might be a good place." She'd done some research on the Internet last night—rather, this morning. She hadn't slept a wink all night. And she'd finally typed the letter to Monsieur Jalbert. "It's the most cosmopolitan city. And I'll be able to come home more often."

"You're not doing this because of my surgery, are you, dear? Because I promise I've got a few good years left in me."

Melissa reached a hand across the table to clasp her mother's. "I know you do, Mom. But no, that's not the reason. I've grown restless in Paris, working with Monsieur Jalbert. He's rather controlling."

"I see."

"I've learned a lot in the time I spent with him, but I've decided enough is enough. After the holidays, I'll go back to Paris and pack up. By then, I will have decided where to set up my business."

"This is exciting news for me, Melissa. I can fly to New York and see you whenever I want to. That'll be terrific!"

"Yeah, and I can come home whenever I want. I can see all the family."

"Yes, that will be lovely. Do you need a loan to start up your company? Because your father and I could—"

"No, Mom, thanks, but I've saved some money over the past six years, plus I have the trust fund Grandpa set up for me. Dad has sent me a statement every year."

"Yes, your father is very good at what he does."

"Does he prefer playing the stock market more than he does ranching?" Melissa asked suddenly. That thought had never occurred to her. Was that why he had turned the ranch over to her brother?

"Actually, I think so. Playing the stock market takes a lot of skill and constant reading, but it also involves the thrill of success. It takes a long year of hard work before a rancher knows if he's been successful. Your father enjoys the excitement of the hunt for a good investment and the more immediate payoff."

"I don't think John realizes that he's doing Dad a favor. Maybe I should mention that to him," Melissa said slowly, considering that idea from all sides.

"Yes, it might be a good plan," Camille said. "I hadn't realized that John was struggling with his father's decision until you said something earlier. It's a good thing you came home for a lot of reasons, dear."

"Thanks, Mom. And please don't tell Dad about my decision just yet."

"No, dear, I—"

The phone rang.

Melissa got up to answer it. "Hello?"

"Hi, it's Harry."

Melissa stepped out of the kitchen as far as the cord would let her. "Hi," she replied, trying to control her breathing.

"I need to ask you a favor."

"Sure." She was so glad to hear from him after yesterday's fiasco, she would've agreed to anything.

"I wondered if you'd join me for dinner at the steak house tonight? Before you say anything I have to tell you it will be surveillance, not a date."

"Oh." Almost immediately her high hopes were dashed.

"We'll be with Mike and Caroline."

"Okay."

"You'll go?" Harry asked, sounding surprised.

"Yes, I will. Shall I come to the Sheriff's Office or meet you at the steak house? And what time?"

"Eight, and come to the office."

"Okay."

"Well…okay." And he hung up the phone.

Melissa hung up, too. Clearly, Harry was still upset about Pierre. But it wasn't her fault. She'd broken her engagement before she came home, and she wasn't going to change her mind about that!

She returned to the table in a pensive mood.

"Something wrong?" her mother asked.

"You might say that. Harry just asked me out to dinner tonight."

"HAVE YOU TALKED TO Melissa?" Mike asked as he came out of his office. "I can get Caro to—"

"I talked to her. She agreed." Harry didn't look up.

"Great. That'll work. Dale, have you found someone?"

"Yeah. Betsy, one of the nurses at the hospital, said she'd help me out. She doesn't work tonight."

"Okay. We're all set here. I hope we get lucky and catch the guy tonight. That would be a real feather in our cap. The boys in Buffalo would never forgive us," Mike said with a grin.

"Uh, yeah, boss, that'll be fine," Harry responded in a bland tone.

"Is something wrong, Harry? When we talked about it earlier, you seemed to think this was a good idea."

"No, it is a good idea! I just— I hope it works."

"We sure don't want a rapist from Buffalo thinking he can move his operation to Rawhide."

"Exactly. We're having a fair number of ladies coming here from Buffalo because of the cowboys pouring into town on the weekends."

"Yeah," Dale agreed. "It's good for business at the steak house, but a serial rapist would ruin it."

Mike nodded. "Okay, be ready at eight. Is Melissa coming here?"

"Yeah, she'll be here," Harry replied. He couldn't believe that the first evening he took Melissa out would be on police business. However, he felt awkward with Pierre in town. And even if the Frenchman wasn't in Rawhide, the fact that Melissa was heading back to France, where Pierre lived, made Harry feel reluctant to kiss her anymore.

He stopped that thought. He *wanted* to kiss Melissa, but he didn't think he should. That was the problem. His conscience wouldn't let him do it. Damn. He guessed it was good that he wouldn't have a chance to.

Shortly before eight that evening, Harry went upstairs and changed his shirt. He put on a holster at the small of his back, then added a corduroy jacket to cover the gun. When he saw Melissa's car pull up, he hurried out of his apartment and down the stairs.

By the time he reached her vehicle, she was already standing beside it. He gave her an awkward greeting. "You, uh, are a couple of minutes early."

"I didn't want to be late."

"Yeah, thanks. I'm sure Mike and Caroline are ready, but we can go inside out of the cold to check on—"

"Hi, guys," Mike said from behind Harry. "You both ready to go?"

"Yes, I think we are," Melissa said.

Harry turned around and nodded to his boss.

"Then let's go have some steaks. I'm starving."

Harry waited until Mike and Caroline had passed him. Then he indicated Melissa should follow the others. He stepped up beside her, but was careful not to touch her.

Once inside the restaurant, Mike led them to an empty table with a Reserved sign on it.

He and Harry took the seats facing the door, while Caroline and Melissa sat opposite them.

The women were chatting about the family when Harry suddenly stood. "I'll be back in a minute."

Melissa had actually forgotten about the surveillance aspect of their evening. She stared after him as he followed a couple out of the restaurant,

"Sorry, Melissa," Mike said. "He'll be back soon."

"Yes, of course."

Caroline drew her attention. "Did you hear we're building a new house?"

"Actually, Harry mentioned it. Are you looking forward to moving?"

Caroline rolled her eyes. "The moving part won't be fun, though many members of the family have volunteered to help us. But I'm excited about the new house. Right now we don't have a lot of room. But I had to give up my home office when we had Sam. Now, with baby Jake, the two boys have to share the second bedroom, and they wake each other up."

"Separate rooms would be nice."

"Most definitely. The new house even has a study for Mike and me to share."

"What are you going to do with your old house?"

"We haven't decided. Maybe we'll rent it out unless someone comes along who wants to buy it."

Harry returned at that moment, slipping into his chair and shaking his head at Mike.

Unable to restrain herself, Melissa reached out and touched his arm. "Did you— I mean—"

"No. Just an amorous couple," Harry said, looking away from her.

"Oh."

Just then Harry noticed that Dale had arrived. Melissa turned around to discover the new deputy escorting Betsy into the restaurant.

Melissa smiled. Then she asked, "Are we going to dance this time, Harry?"

Harry looked at Mike and received a nod of approval. "We'll try, Melissa, but I'm not very good."

"I know. You told me. Go ask them to play a slow song, why don't you?"

"Okay."

Harry crossed the room to where the band was playing. When they finished their song, he offered some money to the band leader and whispered in his ear. Then he came back to Melissa's side. "Ready?"

"Oh, yes," she assured him, following him to the dance floor. When he put his arms around her, he didn't pull her close. That was too dangerous. She slipped her arms around his neck and whispered, "Just sway back and forth, Harry. That will be enough."

But it wasn't. He wanted to wrap her up in his arms and never let her go. But he had to. She was going back to France.

A sudden tap on his shoulder, followed by a French accent, disrupted their dance. "It is my turn, Harry."

Harry backed away from Melissa, ignoring her gaze. "Bring her back to our table when the dance ends," he told Pierre, then he stalked away.

Mike and Caro were dancing, too, so he sat at the table alone. When the waitress served their meals, he started on his.

The music ended then, and Mike and Caroline came back to the table. "Where's Melissa?" Mike asked.

"With Pierre."

After a sharp look at Harry, Mike scanned the dance floor until he found her. She was arguing with Pierre on the other side of the room.

"Stay here with Harry, Caro. I'll go talk to Pierre."

Caroline reached a hand out to touch Harry's arm. "Don't worry. Mike will calm things down."

"Yeah." Harry nodded. "Think he can make Pierre disappear?"

"He can if anyone can," Caroline said with a sympathetic smile. "It doesn't look like Melissa is any happier about Pierre's appearance than you are."

"Maybe." He wasn't going to let his feelings show.

"Looks like all three of them are coming over here," Caroline whispered.

Harry pressed his lips tightly together.

"Pierre asked to join us," Mike said as the trio reached the table. Without saying anything, Pierre pulled up an extra chair between Melissa and Caroline.

Mike elbowed Harry, and he was reminded of their reason for being there. A young couple was leaving. He got to his feet and followed them out. In the floodlights of the parking lot he recognized a cowboy who worked on Griff's ranch. Harry had known him for several years. He returned to the table and shook his head at Mike.

"I'm glad you're back," Melissa whispered.

"You have Pierre to entertain you."

"I don't want Pierre to entertain me!" Melissa retorted, anger building in her voice. "And I've told him that!"

"Yeah, it looks like he's shaking in his boots," Harry drawled.

After the main course Caroline announced she wanted dessert, and Melissa agreed with her.

"Of course you do. You have such a sweet tooth," Pierre teased.

His teasing depressed Harry. He hadn't known Melissa had a sweet tooth. Obviously Pierre knew her better than he did.

After the waitress brought the desserts they'd ordered, Harry sipped his coffee, trying not to show how closely he was watching Melissa and the Frenchman.

Pierre whispered something in her ear, but she shook her head. Finally he got up and asked a young lady to dance with him. Harry let out the breath he'd been holding.

"How long do we have to stay?" Melissa asked him in a whisper.

Harry finally looked at her. "You're ready to leave?"

"Yes. I don't want to spend any more time with Pierre."

After a moment, Harry said, "Mike, do you need us any longer? Melissa wants to go home. Can I escort her to her vehicle and return?"

"Yeah, why don't you do that."

"Okay. I'll be right back."

Harry pulled Melissa's chair from the table and she got up.

"Thanks for the evening," she said to Mike. "I'll see you soon, Caro."

Once they were outside, Melissa slipped her hand through Harry's arm. "Harry, I didn't tell Pierre where I'd be tonight."

"I know. Mike said he'd called the office."

"I just didn't want you to think I invited him there."

"I know."

"So why are you acting like I did something wrong?"

"I'm not—" A woman's shrill scream split the night and Harry's demeanor suddenly turned serious, professional.

"Go get Mike," he told Melissa. "Tell him to come to the alley beside the restaurant." And he ran in that direction.

Melissa did as he asked, sending Mike outside. Dale accompanied him. Betsy and Caroline joined Melissa at the table to await the men's return.

"What's going on?" the nurse asked.

Caroline explained, "They were here on surveillance. There's reason to believe a rapist who's been striking in Buffalo has moved here."

"And they found him?" Betsy asked.

"We don't know," Melissa said. "Harry and I were outside when we heard a woman's scream. He sent me in to get Mike. And then Dale joined them, thank God."

Betsy bobbed her head. "Three on one. Better odds to ensure your guys will be safe."

"Exactly!" Caroline said without hesitation.

Melissa wasn't so sure Harry was "her guy" but she did want him safe.

"I don't blame you," Betsy said, her expression grim. "The other morning at the hospital was scary. I'm glad I'm not taking part in it tonight."

Melissa nodded, and Caroline said, "Yes, definitely."

Suddenly Dale appeared in the doorway and hurried over. "Caroline, Mike wants you to take the woman to the clinic and do a rape kit."

"Oh, the poor thing. Yes, of course." Caroline stood at once.

"I'll go with you," Betsy and Melissa said in unison.

"Good. I think it'll make her feel better."

Melissa couldn't repress her revulsion. "Did you get the bastard?"

Dale nodded. "We'll take the perp over to the jail now to process him." He looked at Betsy. "It'll take about an hour. Will you be at the clinic?"

"Yes. I'll stay there until I hear from you," she said with a blush.

"I'll get there as soon as I can." He dashed out the door again.

Melissa went with Caroline and Betsy to the hospital, accompanying the victim. Then she came back to the restaurant to find the woman's friend and tell her where she was.

After that Melissa returned to the Sheriff's Office to find Harry. There were a number of people milling around, so she moved silently to his side.

"How much longer will you have to work?" she asked him softly.

"I'm not sure."

"Shall I wait?" Melissa asked, hoping for the same enthusiasm that Dale exhibited toward his date.

But Harry barely looked up from his desk. "No, I don't think so. I'll see you soon."

She waited a moment, hoping against hope that he'd change his mind. Then, feeling as if her heart was breaking, she turned and walked out into the cold dark night.

Numbness was her only companion on the ride home. When she entered the house, she found her father waiting up for her.

"You got back early, didn't you?" he asked bluntly.

"So."

"So I expected you to stay until the place closed."

"Harry was busy capturing a rapist," she said, as if that were a normal, everyday occurrence.

"What?" Griff exclaimed, jumping to his feet. "Are you all right?"

"I'm fine. I wasn't involved. I merely assisted Caroline in taking care of the victim."

"Tell me what happened. Did Harry put you in danger?"

"Of course not." She told her father about the evening, up until the victim was taken to the hospital.

"The poor thing was shaking, so I held her hand during the examination. After that, I went to find her friend, and took her to the Sheriff's Office to give some information to Mike. An exciting evening, huh?"

Griff stood and pulled her into a hug. "That's why dads get old fast. They worry about things happening to their daughters."

"Thanks, Daddy," Melissa said, kissing him on the cheek and feeling guilty about the things she excluded from her tale. "I'm tired. I'm going to bed now."

"Okay, no need to get up for breakfast. John and I can manage. You sleep until your mother wakes up." He gave her shoulder a squeeze. "You did a good thing tonight, honey. I'm proud of you."

"Thanks, Dad."

Now she felt doubly guilty. She hadn't come home early because she was a good person, but because Harry didn't want her. Of course, he'd said it was because he was busy, but she knew better. He'd scarcely looked at her all evening. And definitely not since Pierre had joined them. It was as if he'd conceded to Pierre.

But she was not Pierre's for the choosing. Hadn't she

made that clear? All she knew was how much she'd wanted to be in Harry's arms tonight.

But now she lay in her bed, alone.

HARRY STARED AFTER Melissa, long after she'd left the Sheriff's Office. He couldn't allow himself even a kiss. Not anymore.

"Harry?" Mike called.

He spun around, hoping no one had noticed his distraction. He spent another half hour discussing the case with his boss, finishing his work. Then he trudged up the stairs to his apartment.

His empty apartment.

Harry decided he'd been a fool to ever kiss Melissa. He hadn't known anything about her, except that he was drawn to her pouty lips. Now he was paying for his lack of resistance. She was going away in a few weeks, returning to France...and probably to Pierre. She must've been laughing at Harry even as she curled into his arms and lifted her lips to his.

His fingers tightened into fists as he realized how badly he wanted to hold her, to taste her. But he couldn't. He slammed his fist into the sofa.

Finally, he stood and went to his bedroom. He was going to have to find a new girlfriend or go crazy. But he hadn't seen anyone who could compare to Melissa. Maybe he never would.

Chapter Thirteen

"Melissa," a soft voice called.

Melissa jerked to a sitting position, ready to sprint to her mother's room to see what she wanted. Instead, when she opened her eyes, her mother was there in her room.

"Mom! What are you doing up?"

"I got up and fixed breakfast this morning for John and your dad."

"But Dad said he and John would manage on their own," she protested.

"Yes, and then it would've taken all morning to clean up the mess. I've had your father's help before. Besides, he said you needed to sleep in."

"But I should've gotten up."

"Good heavens, child, I've been up and around for several days now. I admit I take a nap sometimes, but there's no reason I can't get up and fix breakfast. I won't break."

"Mom, you're making me feel guilty."

"Nonsense. Come eat your breakfast."

Melissa grabbed her robe and then stepped into the bathroom. When she saw her reflection in the mirror, she stared in horror. Streaks of tears stained her face, and her eyes were red, swollen. With one glance her mother had surely known she'd been crying. Melissa hurriedly rinsed her face and practiced a happy smile in the mirror. Not quite as believable as it needed to be, but it was the best she could do.

She rushed to the kitchen and found her mother sitting at the table with a cup of coffee in front of her. At Melissa's place waited a plate of scrambled eggs and bacon, along with a platter of biscuits.

"I can't eat that many biscuits, Mom!"

"Good. I'll have some to keep you company. Bring me a saucer, would you, please?"

Melissa did as she asked and then sat down and started eating.

"So, how was your date last night?"

Melissa kept her gaze on the scrambled eggs as if they were the most important things in the world. "Fine."

"Uh, I should've said I talked to your father this morning."

"Oh, so he told you about—about the rapist?"

"Yes. Was the victim from Rawhide?"

"No, she was from Buffalo. Can you believe it? The steak house is known in Buffalo as a good place to meet cowboys."

"The ladies of Rawhide have known that for a long time," Camille said with a smile.

"That's not where you met Dad."

"No. I had an inside track, since I was living at the ranch when Griff arrived," Camille said with a sweet smile and a faraway look. "You didn't meet Harry there, either."

"Actually, I did. Remember? My first Friday night home."

"That seems like so long ago. It's only been a week."

"Yes, I guess so. But a lot has happened in that week."

Camille nodded. "Harry is still coming for Sunday dinner, isn't he?"

Damn! Melissa had forgotten she'd invited him. The last thing she wanted now was to face him in front of her parents. "Uh, I forgot to mention it again, what with all the excitement."

"That's okay. John is going to the general store to order some special feed he read about. He can stop in and make sure he's coming. Harry's such a lovely man. I'll enjoy visiting with him."

Her mother had no idea how lovely Harry was. But Melissa knew, every last inch of him. Yet he wasn't interested. Well, maybe for a roll in the hay, but he wouldn't ask her to stay. She supposed he had someone else lined up for when she left!

"Dear? Is anything wrong?" her mother asked.

Melissa looked down at her eggs again. "No, why would you think that?"

Camille chuckled and reached out to touch her hand. "Because you've got what I call that bulldog look on your face. It's one you learned from your father. And it usually means trouble for someone, maybe even yourself."

"I... was just thinking about the ladies I met last night who came into town to catch a cowboy. I don't think that's fair."

"Did Harry flirt with them?"

"Of course not! He was with me."

"Good. That's the way it should be."

WHEN JOHN AND GRIFF CAME in at noon, Melissa had lunch prepared. She hadn't let her mother raise a hand. They all sat down together, enjoying the rare chance of having the whole family together.

Conversation was lively, but Melissa found herself at times distracted.

"Are you feeling all right, dear?" her mother asked. "You're not saying much."

"Oh, yes, Mom. I was just thinking about—about Caroline and Mike's plan to move into their new home. I haven't even seen their old one."

"Oh, it's a darling little house, very close to the Sheriff's Office, on the street behind it. We all pitched in and helped B.J. decorate it before Caroline came home, so she'd have her own place to live."

This week Melissa had learned more about her family then she had in six years. "Oh, really?"

"We completely redid the house. B.J. was emphatic that we put in no girlie frills. From the time she was little, Caroline liked everything classic, with clean lines and bright colors. It was a wonderful house for her."

"I'd like to see it. They said they would either rent it out or sell it, if they got an offer."

"Your mom and I would buy it for you if you want to stay," Griff said.

"Griff!" Camille protested.

"Dad!" Melissa exclaimed.

"How's she going to decide if we don't make an offer?" Griff asked his wife. "She ought to know that she wouldn't have to live at home here with us. I mean, we love her, but we understand her need to be independent."

Camille's lips twitched and so did Melissa's. She understood her father was spouting what her mother had told him. She knew her father wasn't as enlightened as he sounded this morning.

"I appreciate that, Dad. Why don't I go into town with John and visit Caroline? I'll give her a call and see if she's going to be there."

"Good idea, dear," Camille said. "I'm sure she'd love for you to visit. And while you're in town, you can check with Harry about Sunday."

HARRY GOWAN WAS DEPRESSED.

Things had gone badly at the end of the night and he wasn't sure he knew why. He wasn't sure Melissa understood, though. After all, he'd been willing to kiss her whenever she'd mentioned she was leaving.

The only good part of the last twelve-plus hours had

been his routine. It comforted him, made him feel his life was normal again.

Normal, but without Melissa.

He missed her. He thought about calling her, but knew that was the wrong thing to do.

Mike came into the office just as Harry sat down at his desk.

"Morning, Harry. That was good work last night," the sheriff said.

"Thanks, Mike. I got lucky." He regretted those words immediately. They had another connotation, entirely different. And entirely untrue.

"I talked to the police chief in Buffalo. They're sending someone over today to interview our prisoner."

"I doubt they'll get much out of him. He wasn't interested in talking last night."

"We'll see. By the way, have you had lunch?"

"No, I wasn't hungry."

"Good, come join me," Mike said, waiting for Harry to stand up.

"Mike, I'm on duty. I can't leave."

"There are three other deputies here and we'd be two minutes away. Come on."

Harry followed him out of the office. Once they were seated at the café and had given their orders, he eyed Mike assessingly. "Why aren't you eating lunch at home, Mike? Is Caroline working today? It is Saturday, isn't it?"

"No, she's off today. It's Jon's Saturday."

"Then—"

"Oh, Melissa called to ask if she could come visit Caroline. My wife suggested I get lost," Mike added with laughter.

Melissa was in town? Would she stop by the Sheriff's Office? She knew he was on duty. Harry squelched the urge to rush back to his desk in case she dropped in. "Uh, did Caro say why Melissa was coming into town?"

"No, I thought maybe you knew," Mike said, raising one eyebrow.

"No! I have no idea."

Mike stared at him. "You sound pretty down. Did things not go well last night?"

"They went great until the end."

"I meant with Melissa," Mike said.

Harry kept his voice low. "There's nothing between us. She's going back to France."

"You believe that?"

"Why wouldn't I? That's what she's told me every time I got near her."

"I'm wondering. She said that, but she seems to be doing things that indicate she's putting down roots."

"Like what?"

"Caroline said she's promised to take care of her mother. She doesn't think she'll leave her family again. It's been clear they've missed her terribly."

Harry sat there staring into space. Then he said, "She's always told me she plans to return to France."

"You haven't been acting like you believe her."

He shrugged. "I pretended to myself it wasn't true. That she'd change her mind. But she still says it, so I believe her now."

The waitress arrived with their orders, and Mike sat there quietly until she departed.

"Have you told Melissa how you feel about her?"

"Why would I tell her that, since she's leaving?"

"To find out if it might be enough to make her want to stay, Harry. You've got to give her a reason."

"Someone said she'd probably get over her anger with Pierre. They seemed well suited to each other. Did you see them dancing together last night? Did you hear him tease her about having a sweet tooth? I didn't know that about her."

"I don't think those things matter."

"I do."

Both men started eating their lunch, though Harry couldn't even taste his food. He was too busy thinking about Melissa.

Damn! Should he tell her how he felt? He grimaced. Why put his heart out on the counter for her to chop into little bits before she left the country?

"Damn!" he repeated, this time out loud.

"What's wrong, Harry?"

"Did I say something?" he asked warily.

"Yeah, you said 'damn.' Why?"

With a big sigh, Harry said, "I tried not to fall for her, but I just realized I have. I'm in love with Melissa."

"Congratulations!" Mike said with a grin. "Have you decided to tell her?"

Harry blew out a long breath and gave his boss a pensive look. "To tell you the truth, Mike, I don't know."

"OH, CAROLINE, this is great!" Melissa exclaimed when she entered the house.

"It is, isn't it? I wasn't sure until I got here how nice this house would be for me. But now that there are four of us, it's a little small. Besides, we need a housekeeper."

"With both of you working, I guess that would be a help."

"Yes, and it would provide some stability for our children. Sometimes Mike and I both have to respond to the same emergency. That makes it very difficult."

"I hadn't thought of that."

Caro led her into the kitchen, where she poured lemon iced tea and offered Melissa a seat at the table. "It hit me early on. Our first real date was at a French restaurant in Buffalo. A Rawhide lady shot her philandering fiancé right in front of us. Mike handled the shooter and I tended to the dead man's date, who also got shot."

"Wow. That was an even more interesting date than last night."

"Yes. I hope the events last evening didn't spoil things for you and Harry."

"No, they didn't," Melissa said, hoping to keep her voice even. Evidently, though, her cousin was more intuitive than Melissa had thought.

"But something spoiled it?"

She decided to confide in Caroline. "Ever since Pierre arrived, Harry doesn't seem interested."

"I really like Harry," Caroline said softly.

"So do I," Melissa whispered.

Caroline took a sip of her iced tea. After a moment, she said, "Did you ask him why?"

"No, but he's made it clear he isn't interested anymore. Last night he didn't even kiss me good-night. Did Mike ever do that?"

"Yes, at one point he told me to stop feeling sorry for myself, and left me standing there. It made me figure things out." She had a dreamy smile on her face.

Melissa wanted a smile like that. One that told of long nights in a lover's arms, of days spent together, of shared burdens and victories.

But all she'd had were Harry's goodbye kisses.

"Melissa, maybe there's a reason Harry thinks you're going back to Pierre."

"Do you think he believes I would tolerate a man who isn't faithful? I'd never do that."

"I don't think your father would, either."

"I know Dad wouldn't. When he realized Pierre had two-timed me, he told me to get him out of the house," Melissa said, squaring her jaw.

"I think you need to talk to Harry," Caroline stated.

"I'm not sure I can. He's made it clear he's not interested."

"And you don't mind if he moves on?"

Melissa considered the question, and finally said, "Yes, I do."

"So you're in love with him?"

Undeniably. Thoroughly. Irrevocably. Absolutely. She loved Harry Gowan.

"Yes."

The admission didn't seem to shock Caro. She calmly asked, "So what happens to going back to France?"

"I decided yesterday I'm not going back to France, other than to pack up my belongings."

"Really?" Caroline cried with a big smile. "I'm so glad you're coming home!"

"I'm not. I'm thinking of settling in New York."

"Why?"

"I need to sell my jewelry."

"Are you going to personally sell it, not put it in stores?"

Melissa thought about that question. "No, I was going to contact some high-end shops."

"Then why not live here and go to the city when you need to?"

"It's not easy, Caro. I need to hire some interns or workers to help me. It takes time to turn out jewelry, even if I already have designs ready."

"Maybe you could build your workshop on the empty property across the street, and add a couple of apartments over it. Let the internship include a place to live."

Melissa had to admit the suggestion was a good one. "That's an idea, assuming I find the right people."

"And you could rent or buy this place. It would be perfect!"

Melissa looked at Caroline. "You're not just saying that to sell this house, are you?"

"No. But I'd like it to go to someone who would love it."

"That would be easy to do. I guess you'll be taking the furniture with you?"

"Not really. The new house is much larger, and we've decided to furnish it with new furniture. Except for the paintings and those lamps," Caroline said, pointing to the living room. "Otherwise, we'd be glad to include the furniture if the new owner wanted it."

Melissa debated her answer. She had to admit that not only did her cousin's idea sound appealing, it seemed thoroughly workable. She longed to have the type of happy life Caroline had found in this house. But could she live here without Harry? Could she live in his town without having him beside her?

And could she live here and make her jewelry, as Caroline had suggested? Why hadn't she realized that? That she could have a workshop here and sell to the American market?

Frequent plane trips would be warranted, to New York and San Francisco, Seattle and Dallas—all the major cities—but she wasn't opposed to travel. It'd still give her a taste of the sophisticated lifestyle she'd enjoyed the past six years.

But the biggest plus was how close she'd be to her

family. She wouldn't have to hear the stories of their lives; she'd share them.

She looked at her cousin, who regarded her expectantly.

"Caroline, I want it. I want to build a workshop across the street like you suggested. But could you not tell anyone, even Mike, for a while? Until I figure out what's going on with Harry."

"So you won't want it if—"

"I want it no matter what, but I don't want Harry to marry me unless he loves me, unless he can't stand to let me go. If he knows I'm staying, he may just think I'm convenient."

"I think you're wrong about Harry, but I won't tell Mike until I have to. I'm thrilled that you want to buy my house. I'll keep the price low."

"*I* won't be buying it. Dad promised to buy it for me as a gift," Melissa said with a giggle. "So price it however you planned. He can afford it!"

Caroline laughed with her. "Boy, he really does want you to stay, doesn't he?"

Chapter Fourteen

It didn't take Harry long to realize he wanted to talk to Melissa. But it was too late to casually drop in at Caroline's.

He was too restless and fidgety to remain at his desk. Instead, he propped himself against a post out on the sidewalk in front of the office, watching the citizens of Rawhide pass by, greeting them all by name.

He'd been out there at least half an hour when John Randall walked up.

"Hi, John," Harry said with a smile, hoping his friend was still talking to him.

"Hey, Harry. Have you seen Melissa?"

"No, I haven't. Mike said she was having a visit at Caroline's."

"Oh. I just knew Mom told her to stop by and remind you about Sunday dinner. She said she's really looking forward to visiting with you."

His heart beat faster. "Melissa said that?"

"No," John said with a laugh. "Mom said that."

His pulse rate slowed back to normal. "Well, I wouldn't want to disappoint your mom. She's a sweet lady."

John nodded in agreement. "I'll tell her you said that." He pulled a cell phone out of his coat pocket. "Excuse me while I see where Melissa is."

Harry stood there, pretending not to listen as John spoke into the device. "When are you coming…? Okay, I'll meet you at the truck."

He turned off the phone. "She's on her way now."

"Where are you parked?"

He nodded down the street. "By the general store. I'll just wait here until she comes by."

"Good. I'll enjoy the company."

"What are you doing out here, anyway? Don't you know it's cold?"

"It's not so bad in the sun, and I get to visit with a lot of people I don't see during the week."

"That's true. And you don't work on Sunday."

"Yeah," Harry said, looking the other way to check if Melissa was coming.

"I'll tell you when I see her," John said with a grin. "That way you don't have to throw your back out trying to spot her first."

Harry's cheeks flushed as he muttered, "Thanks."

After a minute, John said, "You two didn't have an argument, did you?"

"I don't think so."

"Melissa can be hard to understand. Mom says it's because she and Dad are a lot alike."

"I don't think that's our problem, I think it has something to do with Pierre," Harry said dryly.

John stared at him. "I don't think she's interested in him."

"Maybe not now, but she's going back to France, where he'll be."

"Yeah. I don't like the idea, but she still seems to be planning to do that." John's expression turned serious. "We'd all like for Melissa to come back home." Then he said, "Uh-oh. Here she comes now—and look who's with her."

Harry fought the desire to turn and gaze at her. It seemed a long time since he'd seen her, though in reality it was just last night.

Before he could give into his urges, Mike stepped outside the office.

"Hey, John. You helping Harry pass the time?" he asked with a smile. Then, following the young man's gaze, he noticed the Frenchman walking with Melissa. "What the heck…?"

Harry turned then and his eyes zeroed in on Melissa, who looked radiant in a navy peacoat with a bright fuchsia scarf and mittens. Unfortunately, she had another accessory. Pierre de Leon.

Harry could feel his blood boil.

He held on to his temper as the duo made their way toward the Sheriff's Office.

Melissa smiled as she greeted him. "Hello, Harry," she said, neglecting the other two men. "If you're still coming to dinner tomorrow after church, would you mind giving Pierre a ride? He's not sure he can find his way by himself."

Harry looked at Pierre and prayed his eyes weren't shooting the daggers he wanted to thrust at the man. "I thought you were leaving tomorrow."

"*Mais oui,* but my flight does not take off until seven in the evening."

"Then I'd be glad to give you a ride," Harry said through clenched teeth.

Melissa sent him a brilliant smile. "Good. I'll wait for you in the truck, John. It's rather cold out today."

With that, she walked away.

The four men stood there, none of them knowing what to say, until Pierre broke the silence.

"I shall meet you at what time?" he asked innocently.

Either the man was that dumb, or he was rubbing Harry's nose in it. Still, Harry had promised Melissa.

"Be here at twelve-fifteen, or else I'll leave without you." He'd drive him, but he didn't have to be nice.

"Then I will bid you goodbye." Pierre turned and strolled down the street before Harry realized the arrogant guy hadn't even said thanks.

"I hear he has a date tonight," Mike said.

"With Melissa?" Harry asked despondently.

"Nope. With a young woman he met last night at the steak house after Melissa and you left."

"She doesn't know, does she?"

John frowned. "Maybe I should tell her."

"I don't think you should," Harry said. "You don't want to break her heart, do you?"

"I want her to know what she's getting into if she links up with that Pierre!" He said goodbye and followed his sister to his truck.

After John walked away, Mike asked, "You okay?"

"Yeah, I guess so. You know how it is when a woman messes with your mind."

Mike laughed. "You got that right."

JOHN GOT INTO THE TRUCK and slammed his door.

Melissa knew he was letting her know he wasn't happy with her. "What?"

"I'm just telling you now, little sister. When Harry comes to Sunday dinner, you'd better mind your manners and not flirt outrageously with Pierre!"

"When have you ever seen me flirt outrageously with Pierre?"

"I haven't, but I didn't expect you to invite him to Sunday dinner either."

"He invited himself, John. What was I to do?"

Her brother shook his head. "What's going on with you and Harry anyway?"

"Nothing."

"Yeah, right." John threw the truck into gear and backed out of his parking spot. "You can explain it to Mom if you don't mind your manners. She won't accept that kind of answer."

"I can't explain, John. Please," Melissa said, unable to hold back a few tears that slid down her cheeks.

He looked at her and then pulled to a stop at the side of the road. "I'm sorry, sis," he said, and reached out to wipe them away. "Did Harry do something he shouldn't? Do I need to go talk to him?"

Melissa smiled as she rubbed away more tears. "No, he didn't do anything I didn't ask him to do. But I don't think he's serious about—about us. And it h-hurts."

"He told you that?"

"Yes, but not in so many words. I—I could just tell."

After he pulled back onto the road, John said, "If it helps any, Harry's still interested."

"You talked about us?" Melissa said.

"Hell, yeah! We all want you to stay. We miss you, sis."

Melissa buried her face in her hands.

"Did I mess up?"

Melissa, who was crying again, shook her head. "No, I just— I want a marriage like Mom and Dad have."

"And you can't have that with Harry?"

"I could. If he wanted to marry me no matter what. But if he married me because I'm a Randall and it's convenient, it would be a disaster."

"You think Harry is like that? I don't."

"You weren't there, John."

"No, I won't argue that, but I think he's in love with you."

Melissa just closed her eyes. thinking how amazing it would be if that were true.

AFTER DINNER THAT NIGHT, John pulled his mother aside. "Uh, Mom, did Melissa tell you Pierre is coming for dinner tomorrow?"

"Along with Harry?" Camille asked. "Why?"

"She claims he invited himself."

"I see." Camille hesitated as she brought the coffee mug to her lips. "That won't be a good combination—Pierre and Harry."

John nodded. "She and Harry are having problems. And Mike told us that Pierre has a date tonight with a woman he met at the steak house last night. Should I tell Melissa that?"

"No, dear, I don't think that's necessary."

"Melissa seems to think Harry is dating her because she's convenient. I don't read him that way at all."

"No, and I think he could've found other women much more convenient than Melissa." Camille seemed to be in deep thought, so John waited.

"I'll see what I can figure out tomorrow, Son."

"Okay, Mom."

Camille went to her room to get ready for bed. Her husband followed her.

"What are we going to do about Melissa?" Griff asked.

"Oh, I don't know. Why don't you promise to give her all our money if she'll come home?"

"What? That's crazy!"

She gave him a knowing look. "I thought so."

"Aw, Camille, the house won't be that much, and John has the ranch. It seemed more than fair to me."

"It is, dear. I just wanted to make sure you didn't get carried away," she said with a smile. "Actually, I think she's going to make some changes."

Griff's face lit up. "You think so?"

"Yes, but I don't know if she'll take you up on your offer. She may move to New York City. She hasn't quite decided yet."

"I could offer Harry—"

"No! Enough trying to manipulate your children or anyone else. You have to have faith that they'll do the right thing. That's why you turned the ranch over to John, isn't it? Because you had faith he would do the right thing? I think you owe that to Melissa more than any amount of money."

Griff hung his head. "Yeah, I guess I haven't done as good a job with Melissa, but I don't understand her work, and she's been too far away to convince me of anything."

"I know. And she may go away again. We just have to wait until she makes up her mind."

HARRY PUT ON A DARK green dress shirt and black slacks for Sunday dinner. He was nervous about going to visit Melissa's family for a lot of reasons. The most important one was that Melissa didn't want him there.

He guessed she'd made her decision. Otherwise, why would she have invited Pierre to come to dinner, too? In fact, Harry should offer to drive the Frenchman out there and then come back home to his apartment. That would make her happy.

Squaring his shoulders, he changed his mind. He'd been invited first. He was going to stay for dinner. If she didn't want him there, she'd have to tell him. Face-to-face.

But he hoped she didn't tell him that. He wanted to spend time with her, even surrounded by her family and Pierre. Damn, Harry was one sick puppy to accept that kind of torture.

With a sigh, he went downstairs to wait for the Frenchman.

Harry was still hoping that he and Melissa could— Could what? That he could convince her not to go back to France and her boyfriend? That wasn't likely.

Unfortunately, Pierre showed up outside the Sheriff's Office at exactly twelve-fifteen.

By the time they reached their ranch, Harry was fed up with the man and his attitude. When he got out of his truck, he saw John coming out to meet him. Uh-oh. Had they changed their mind and no longer wanted him at dinner?

John reached out to shake his hand. "Glad you made it."

"So it's still all right?"

"Absolutely! Mom even made a special dessert for you. And Pierre," he added.

"She didn't need to do that."

"Hello, Pierre," John said, offering his hand.

Pierre shook it briefly. "May we enter?" he asked.

"Yes, of course."

John and Harry followed him to the house.

"I shouldn't have come," Harry muttered. "Melissa doesn't want me here."

"Oh, yeah? Then why did she cry when I tried to talk to her about you two?"

"She did?"

John nodded and held the door open.

Inside, they found Griff already sitting at the head of the table, glowering at Pierre, while the two ladies brought in platters of delicious-smelling food.

Griff stood up and shook Harry's hand, then invited him to sit opposite Pierre, on his left.

After hanging up his hat, Harry greeted both Melissa and Camille before he sat down. "Something sure smells good."

"Of course it does. My mother is one of the best cooks in the county," Melissa said crisply.

Pierre smiled at Melissa. "And we will have wine?

Camille looked upset. "Oh, dear, I didn't think to get you any wine, Pierre. I'm so sorry."

Harry remembered the bottle Melissa had been drinking the night he'd stayed over after rounding up the herd, but she'd poured that out the next morning.

"Pierre will drink coffee, Mom," Melissa said quickly.

"But, *ma chère,* I would rather—"

"No, Pierre!" After serving him coffee, she took the seat beside Harry, leaving her brother to sit beside Pierre.

Conversation was a bit forced at times during dinner,

as Melissa refused to talk with Pierre about her plans for her return to France.

Everyone else chatted determinedly and kept eating, as if hoping the meal would end quickly.

When Camille brought out the dessert, Harry couldn't believe his eyes. "Is that Red's famous chocolate cake?"

"Yes, it is. He gave us his secret recipe this year," she announced with a smile.

"This is a secret?" Pierre asked looking with disdain at the cake. "In France, we are famous for our pastries."

"Red's chocolate cake is better," Melissa snapped.

"*Mais non, chérie.* That cannot be true."

Camille served everyone a piece of cake. When she got to Pierre, he shook his head. "Don't you want some of my dessert?" she asked.

"*Non,* I prefer cheese and fruit."

"Mom doesn't have cheese and fruit, and it's wrong of you to ask for something she hasn't offered!" Melissa glared at her former fiancé.

"I am glad I'm returning to France. This is a barbaric country! There is no wine, no bottled water, and now no cheese and fruit for dessert! I do not like it here."

"I'm glad you're leaving, too, because you are rude and childish. I don't know how I ever thought you would be good husband material!"

"We will discuss our plans when you return to France, *ma chère!* Not here in front of these…people!" Pierre said.

"These people are my family and a friend, Pierre.

And we won't discuss anything when I return to France, because I'll be packing to come home for good!"

As if she'd set off a bomb, both Pierre and her father jumped to their feet, one protesting and one celebrating.

Harry sat there stunned. She was staying? What had made her change her mind? Of course, that didn't mean she'd return to Rawhide, but who knew? Maybe she'd come home more often, at least. Would that be enough for him?

No, it wouldn't.

He stood up, seeing the discomfort on his hostess's face. "Camille, why don't you save my piece of cake for another time, and I'll take Pierre back into town? We don't want him to miss his flight."

"Oh, bless you Harry, that would be wonderful."

"Come on, Pierre," Harry announced, speaking loudly to be heard over the other men's voices. "Time for you to go." He grabbed his arm and began dragging him toward the door.

"*Non!* I must speak to Melissa!"

"I think you've already said too much." Harry kept moving to the door. Griff got up to assist him, hustling Pierre from behind.

Harry was half afraid Pierre might turn around and fight Melissa's dad when they got outside. He probably figured Griff's age would slow him down. Harry tried to hide the smile that thought induced.

Once he got Pierre in his truck, he hurried around to

the driver's side and sped toward Rawhide. Though it wasn't a long trip, it took longer than he liked, with Pierre yelling at him nonstop in both English and French. Harry parked in front the Sheriff's Office, and Pierre jerked open his door.

"I will not forget this, *jamais!*"

"Okay. Have a good flight." Harry even managed to offer a friendly smile.

Pierre growled before he stalked across the street to Dale's apartment. Harry was pretty sure Dale was working, so he wouldn't have to warn him about his angry guest.

With a rueful chuckle, Harry wandered up stairs to his own place. He didn't have anything planned for the rest of the day, but at least he didn't have to think of Melissa going back to France with Pierre.

That didn't stop Harry from missing her.

THE STUNNED SILENCE was broken when Griff came back into the dining room. Taking a deep breath, Melissa slumped down in her chair.

"Child, you're *not* going back to France?" he asked.

"No, Dad, I'm not. And definitely not taking up with Pierre again!"

"You might have told Dad that," John interjected. "I was afraid he was going to have a heart attack when Pierre walked in today."

Griff didn't respond. He headed straight to his daughter, bent down and wrapped his arms around her.

"I'm so glad you got rid of that man," he said. "And I'm glad you're not going back to Europe."

After hugging her father, Melissa said, "Will you be glad to hear I'm staying here in Rawhide? Remember, it will cost you the price of Caroline's house." She gave him a wide smile.

"Baby girl, I don't care about the money. Your mother and I will be so happy to have you living nearby!" He sat down at the table. "I believe I'd like another piece of Red's cake to celebrate."

Ignoring him, Camille asked her daughter, "But, dear, can you make your jewelry here? I would hate for you to give up your career."

"Yes, Mom. Caro had a great idea—for me to build a workshop on land near the house and add two apartments upstairs for the people who work for me."

"That's super, Melissa!" John beamed at her. "That way you can be a jeweler *and* a cowgirl."

Melissa smiled at her brother. "I don't think I'll be much of a cowgirl, but I'll be able to come out and ride every once in a while."

"Anytime you want, little sister," he said with a grin. Then he asked the one question she didn't have an answer for. "What's going on between you and Harry?"

"I don't know."

"I think you should marry him!" Griff said, a smile on his face.

"Even if he doesn't love me, Dad?"

"What's wrong with you, girl? He's been kissing you all over town!"

"That might've been partly my fault." She didn't want to look up and face her father, but she finally did. And he was staring at her as if she was crazy.

"Griff," her mother said, "I think she's worried that Harry is interested in her because she's a Randall."

"So he should be! Anyone's lucky to land a Randall. But Harry is as honest as they come. He wouldn't lie about loving you, honey." Griff said

Everyone sat silent for a long moment.

Finally, Griff got up and cut his own piece of cake. Then he sat down and ate a forkful. "So what are you going to do about Harry, Melissa? Have you told him you're staying in town?"

"No."

"Are you going to stay even if he isn't interested?" Camille asked, her hands pressed together.

"Yes, Mom, I'm staying. I'll have to travel, especially to get started, but I'll be living here. I'm home."

"I'm so glad Melissa. I think when you tell Harry that, everything will work out."

"Yes, but it's a little awkward to say, 'Hi, Harry, I'm staying. Did you mean it when you kissed me?' Because he hasn't said he loves me. And I won't settle for less."

John joined his father in a second dessert. Through a full mouth he said, "Josh told me Harry was attracted to you before he knew you were a Randall."

Melissa gave her brother a skeptical look. "How would Josh know that?"

"Remember when Harry was looking for a dance partner for you, at the steak house that night? He told Josh there was this knockout who needed a partner."

"I know exactly how you can approach him without any awkwardness," Camille said.

Melissa turned to stare at her mother. "How?"

She pointed to the chocolate cake in the middle of the table. "Harry asked me to save him a piece of cake so he could get Pierre out of here. It would be thoughtful of you to take it to him. I'll cover it in plastic wrap." She stood up from the table to do just that.

"Maybe I should wait until tomorrow," Melissa said apprehensively.

"No," Griff declared. "We're all sitting here worrying about it. I think you should go now."

Melissa rolled her eyes. "I should settle my love life so *you* won't worry? That's a little strange, Dad."

"No," he said, using his fork to make the point, "it's so you won't lose your nerve."

Once again her father was right.

Chapter Fifteen

Melissa slowly climbed the stairs, carrying the large piece of cake her mother had cut for Harry. She thought about checking downstairs for him, but decided not to. She'd rather face him alone, so she was going to take the chance that he was at home.

She knocked on his apartment door and stood there waiting, relieved when she heard footsteps.

Harry swung open the door, surprise on his face when he saw her. "Melissa! Is everything all right?"

"Yes, thanks to your ushering Pierre out of the house so quickly. I came to say thank you and to offer you the chocolate cake you sacrificed."

"That piece looks big enough to share. How 'bout it?"

Melissa looked at the cake. She hadn't realized her mother had cut a piece big enough for two. Obviously, her mom was way ahead of her in planning romantic encounters. "I'd love some," she told Harry.

"Come on in."

Melissa didn't hesitate, until she saw Harry peer down the stairs. "What are you looking for?"

"Your dad. Shouldn't he be showing up about now?"

She chuckled, which helped her relax. "Don't worry. Mom's got him under control."

"That's good news. I was glad to hear you say you weren't going back to France, by the way," he stated as he shut the door. "Where will you be setting up your jewelry company?"

Melissa waited to answer until she was settled on the sofa. "I'm thinking about somewhere locally."

"Really? Would there be much of a market around here?"

"Oh, I didn't mean I'd sell only locally. I'd make the jewelry here, but sell it other places. I'm thinking Neiman Marcus might be a good company to offer it. They have a number of stores now, even in Denver."

Harry stared at her, surprise on his face. "You're— you're really going to make your jewelry here?"

"Why not?"

"Did your father talk you into this?" he asked, suddenly scowling at her.

"No. It was my decision."

"But why?"

"I just hadn't thought of moving home. But when I saw Caroline's house, I knew I wanted it. She suggested I could build a workshop on the land across the street and add a couple of apartments on top. Then I could bring some workers here and have a place for them to live."

"Does she own that land?"

"No, but she thinks I can buy it. I'll have to find out that information on Monday."

Harry didn't say anything.

Melissa took a deep breath. "Are you unhappy that I'm staying in town?"

That question seemed to stun him. After a moment, he said, "Absolutely not. I just want it to be your decision."

"It is." To break the awkward silence that ensued, she asked, "Are you going to share the cake?"

Since he was still clutching the plate, she hoped that would break the tension.

"Oh! Yeah, sure. I'll—I'll cut it in half." He walked over to the kitchen part of the big room. "So you won't be going back to France?"

"I'll have to go pack up my things and talk to Monsieur Jalbert. He won't be happy, but my contract expires at the end of the year, so he has no hold on me."

"And you won't miss…uh, your friends and—and the museums?"

"I'm not saying I won't ever return to France, Harry. I might need to revisit the museums for inspiration. But not that often. And I can invite my friends to come see me." When he turned to stare at her, she immediately said, "Not Pierre."

He went back to cutting the cake. Then he brought over the two plates and forks.

"Can you believe Red has given up his secret cake recipe?" Melissa murmured.

"No, I was surprised. Why did he do that?"

"I asked Mom that question. I was afraid he had some terrible disease and didn't have long to live. But she said he just realized he was getting on up there and didn't want the recipe to die with him. Mildred gave us her cinnamon bun recipe, too."

"Did they give them just to you and Camille?"

"Oh, no, they gave them to all the second generation moms, and said they could share them with their daughters when they married. But I'm the last one not married, so Mom shared them with me anyway."

"Those recipes can be a real temptation to men after they taste them."

Melissa peeped at him from under her thick lashes. "Do they tempt you?"

He cleared his throat. "Uh, yeah, but I'm easy."

"What do you mean?"

"I think I need some water," Harry said, standing. "Do you want some?"

"No, but I'd like to know what you meant."

He ignored her words and crossed over to the sink. After pouring a glass of water, he stood there, holding on to the counter as if it were a lifeline. Finally, he said, "Honey, I've been tempted ever since I saw you. I don't need any 'pastries' as Pierre called them, to be tempted by you."

Melissa put down her piece of cake and followed him to the sink. But she wasn't looking for water. She stopped in front of him. "Then why aren't you doing anything about it?"

He moved away. "Because I'm pretty sure if I touched you, I'd lose control. And it looks like your dad isn't going to rescue you today."

Her eyes lit up at his words. She'd hoped he'd still wanted her, but she hadn't been sure. "I don't want to be rescued today."

Harry broke eye contact and took in a deep audible breath, then let it out with a sigh. "I think we'd better finish the cake."

"That might be dangerous."

His brows furrowed in puzzlement. "What do you mean?"

"I've heard that Red's cake is quite an aphrodisiac," Melissa said in a husky voice.

Harry, who had been walking back to the sofa, stopped in his tracks. "Um, I see. I—I think I'll keep my piece for later."

"Really?" she said, pursing her lips in a pout, as she'd done when she'd first spoken to him in the steak house.

"Don't do that!"

"What?" she asked, her eyes rounding in mock innocence.

"That thing with your lips."

"Why?"

"Because I'm going to lose control!"

"Why don't you?"

"Because you would regret it. I'm not…good enough for a Randall."

Putting her hands on her hips, she stared at him. "Then why were you kissing me all over town?"

"Because you were leaving. There was no danger that—that I'd lose my heart and risk getting it broken." He stood with his head down, like a horse that had been ridden to the point of exhaustion.

Melissa stepped closer to him. "What if I lost my heart, too?"

He stared at her. "Don't play tricks on me, Melissa. If sex is all you want, I know some guys who would oblige you. But—but I can't…"

"Can't what?"

"I can't make love to you and let you go. I'd expect more than a one-night stand. I'd expect something to last a lifetime. And that's the only way I'm going to have sex with you!" His hands were on his hips as he faced her with his ultimatum.

With a saucy smile on her lips, she said, "Okay."

"Okay what?"

"A lifetime seems long enough to me."

"Melissa, I—"

Before he could say anything else, she flew into his arms, eager to erase the pain in his eyes. "Harry, do I have to beg you to love me? Because I will. I want a lifetime with you and no one else."

He wrapped his arms around her and tasted those pouty lips he adored. After a moment, he said, "Are you sure? I'm only a deputy sheriff. I don't make that much money and—"

"I'm not marrying you for your money, Harry."

"But people will think I'm marrying you for yours! That might be hard to take."

She crossed her hands at the back of his neck and stepped even closer until there was nothing between them, not even air. "How about we marry just because we love each other? Mike and Caroline are making it work."

"Yeah, but Mike makes more than me."

Melissa gave him a crooked smile. "So you think it's Mike's money that's paying for that house?"

"The new one? Well, I assumed— You don't think he is?"

"No. Even for Rawhide, that's an expensive place. But it's what they need to take good care of their children. And that's what matters. No one says anything about them, do they?"

"No, because everyone can see that Mike's crazy about Caro. And vice versa."

Melissa brought her lips within a hairs breadth of his. "I'm crazy about you, Harry Gowan. Are you crazy about me?"

"Of course I am, but—"

"I've never had to work this hard in my life to get a man to kiss me!" she exclaimed with a sigh.

"I did kiss you!"

"Well can you kiss me again? It's been so long, I forgot what it feels like." Actually, that couldn't be further from the truth. Melissa remembered every one of Harry's kisses—out on the sidewalk, in his apartment. She could never forget them.

He tightened his hold on her and, his chocolate eyes never leaving hers, brought his lips down slowly, millimeter by millimeter. By the time they touched hers, Melissa was about to melt in a pool at his feet.

At first the kiss was soft and tender, then, with little urging, he deepened it, his tongue darting out to dance with hers. She moaned into his mouth, all the pent-up longing escaping in one heartfelt whoosh.

"Oh, Harry," she rasped when he broke away, "you are a wonderful kisser."

He grinned at her, and she noticed a dimple in his right cheek she'd never seen before. She suspected that for the rest of her days she'd be discovering new things about this man, she looked forward to every one.

"You're not bad yourself," he teased.

She pretended annoyance. "Not bad? I rate you a ten, and you give me…what? A five?" But she couldn't hold back her smile. "Come here, deputy. Let's try it again."

"Damn, woman, you're tempting me!"

She pulled his head down. "I'm trying my best. Is it working?"

"Oh, yeah." With one swift motion, he swept her off her feet and into his arms, then strode away, carrying her to his bedroom.

Melissa had to admit she liked a man of action. She wrapped her arms around him and settled her head in the crook of his neck. She could hardly believe this was about to happen, when yesterday she'd almost given up all hope. She smiled against his woodsy-smelling skin. "I thought it would take more than kisses to convince you, Harry."

"I'm convinced, sweetheart. I've been convinced ever since the first night I saw you, sitting by yourself in the bar." Not breaking stride, he met her eyes. "I love you, Melissa. For a lifetime, forever. Do you love me?"

Her heart was pounding so hard, she reasoned it was good that she was in his arms; her legs wouldn't hold her at the moment. Other men had said those three little words to her, but none had had the effect that he did. "Oh, yes, Harry, I do love you. I thought I was just playing a game, but I soon found out I needed your kisses to survive."

"Well, I definitely want you to survive, so here." He kissed her then, never breaking contact as he put her down at the foot of his bed.

Melissa soon realized she needed more than Harry's kisses; she needed all of him.

As their kisses grew more heated, she reached out to his shirt, undoing one button at a time and allowing her hot breath to trail down over his exposed skin. She could feel the heavy pounding of his heart, matching her own.

Harry grabbed her hands before they could reach the bottom button, tucked into his slacks. "My turn," he whispered. And he proceeded to do the same to her.

When he exposed the top swells of her breasts, he lingered there a moment, cupping them in his big, sure hands. Those hands were about to slip the blouse from her shoulders when suddenly they came to an abrupt halt.

"What is it, Harry? Is something wrong?"

His eyes looked nearly tortured when he finally raised them to hers. Even in the dim room she could see the emotion on his face. "I want to make love to you—"

"I want it, too." She reached out to him.

He sidestepped, running a hand through his thick hair. "But I keep picturing your father, imagining him barging through my door, coming to claim you." He shook his head. "I just keep thinking that, even though you say he was matchmaking, he sure has worked hard to keep us apart." Harry looked at her again. "What if he doesn't want you to marry me?"

She heard the anguish in his voice, the uncertainty. But she knew there was no need for it. "So there's the phone," she said, pointing to it on his bedside table. "Call him and find out."

Harry looked incredulous. "You want me to ask your father if it's okay to make love to you? Melissa, he'll come after me with a shotgun!"

She couldn't help but laugh, in spite of his seriousness. "Not if you tell him you're going to marry me."

He took a moment to debate. Then he nodded. "I guess so." Walking to the phone, he stopped and turned around to look at her. "And you're sure?"

"Oh, yes!"

He dialed the number at the ranch, and over the phone, Melissa heard her father's deep voice answer.

"Griff, I, uh…sorry to bother you, but there was something I needed to tell you." Harry wasted no time changing that last part. "Ask you." Taking a deep breath, he said in a rush, "I'd like your permission to marry Melissa. I hope you and Camille will approve."

Just hearing those words made Melissa warm inside. She stepped next to him, flinging her arms around him and hugging him to her.

There were raised voices on the other end of the line, then she finally heard her father say clearly, "That's perfect, Son. When's the date?"

Harry covered the mouthpiece with his hand and looked down at her. Relief found a home on his face. "Your dad wants to know the date."

"I hadn't even thought of that." Frantically she went through the calendar in her mind. "I—I have to go back to Paris…I'd really like for you to come with me. That could be our honeymoon."

"So should I tell him we'll marry after Christmas?" Harry looked eager to get off the phone now.

"Or we could go between Thanksgiving and Christmas. How about that?" she asked him.

He leaned down for a quick kiss. "I'd like that better. I don't think I'm going to be able to keep my hands off you in public for too long."

She smiled at him. "Me, neither. We can make the

announcement at Thanksgiving dinner, assuming everyone doesn't know by then."

Harry told Griff what they'd decided. "Would that be all right?"

"Let me tell Camille," Griff said, and covered his receiver in turn. "She says that'll be perfect, but she'd have to get started at once. How about the Sunday after Thanksgiving?"

"You'll have to ask Melissa." Harry handed her the phone.

"Mom, are you going to be all right with this? I don't want you to overdo," she said worriedly.

"I'm fine. With a wedding to plan, I'll be even better." She went to talking about details, as if she'd already been planning this day in her head.

But Melissa was having a hard time following her mother. Harry had begun to remove her blouse.

He tugged it off one shoulder, then bent to kiss the skin there. His free hand roamed her back, tracing slow, seductive circles, until it stopped at her bra. Deftly he snapped it open, and Melissa nearly shrieked into the phone.

She cleared her throat. "Uh, Mom, I have to go now. We'll talk more when I get home."

"When should we expect you, dear?" her mother asked.

Melissa looked at Harry and saw the desire in his gaze. "Morning, I think. Bye." Without hesitation she dropped the phone in its charger and went into his arms.

"What about the morning?" Harry asked as he shed her blouse and bra.

"Mom wanted to know when I'd be— Oh, yes," she moaned as he cupped her breasts and kissed each one.

"When you'd what?" His breath was hot on her body.

"When I'd be home." She went back to work on his clothes, pushing his shirt over his shoulders.

"So you're staying the night?"

"Am I not invited?" she teased, looking up at him with a pout.

"Oh, yeah. That just means I can take my time and do this properly, Melissa Randall-soon-to-be-Gowan."

"Hmm," Melissa said dreamily, "I think I'll name my company MRG. That'll be perfect."

"Yes, it will," he agreed as he slid down the zipper of her jeans. Stepping back, he lowered them inch by agonizing inch, running his palms down her legs until he pulled the pants off completely.

Standing there only in her panties, she looked down at him crouched on the floor. "Why am I almost bare and you still have on all your clothes?"

"Because I work faster than you?" he asked with a grin.

She reaching out for him then, and when he stood, she stripped him in the same torturous way he'd done her. When they were both naked, Harry took it upon himself to explore every inch of her body. "Oh, Harry, I—" She gasped as he took her nipple into his mouth and sucked. "Yes, there."

"That's right, sweetheart. Tell, me what you like."

"I like you, Harry. Just you."

He looked up at her, his gaze intent. "I thought you *loved* me," he teased.

"I do love you. I was talking about what I liked…in bed."

He swooped her up once again. "Then let's get in bed." Laying her down on his comforter, he let his eyes rake every inch of her. And she did the same. Everyone had told her that Harry was so modest. Well, there was nothing modest about him. Now he stood there, letting her look.

That day in the workout room was nothing compared to this. Then she'd only glimpsed his broad, muscular chest. Now she got to feast on it. And all the rest of him.

He opened a bedside drawer and took out a foil-wrapped package.

It dawned on Melissa then that they'd never talked about children.

"Do you want to have kids, Harry?" she blurted.

He let out a laugh. "I do, but not right now."

"Me, too. I want a whole bunch of them. But I'd like to wait until I get my company up and running."

"That's what I figured." He took care of the protection and joined her on the bed, taking her in his arms again. "We've got lots of time to talk and plan, Melissa. For now, we have other things to do."

She smiled. "That's what I like about you, Harry. You have your priorities in order." She reached up to him, and this time he took her places she'd never been before. In no time she needed more of him, all of him.

Harry leaned back as he entered her, watching her as

he sheathed himself inside her. And her own gaze never wavered. Though it'd been little more than a week since they'd met, it seemed as if she'd waited forever to be with Harry Gowan, and she wasn't going to close her eyes and miss a minute of it.

She hung on to him, matching his rhythm, and called out his name in a breathless gasp as they climaxed together. She wondered then what it would be like making love to Harry when they'd actually gotten to know each other's bodies. Could it be better than this?

Harry hoisted himself on his elbows, gazing down at her and stroking her face with his thumbs. "Are you okay?" he asked.

"Oh, yeah."

He leaned over and kissed her lips. "I love your lips, by the way."

"I love yours, too. And every other part of you."

"I'm glad you told your mother you'd be spending the night. I don't think I want to leave this bed till morning." He grinned then as she started to move her hips again in an enticing pattern. "I think I may need a few minutes," he admitted, looking at her with twinkling eyes.

But Melissa knew better. She could feel him growing hard already. Still, she teased, "Or you could always go to the chocolate cake."

SOMETHING DISTURBED Harry's sleep. He opened his eyes to find Melissa next to him, one arm and leg wrapped over him, holding him close. He decided he liked waking up that way.

Then the phone rang again and he reached over her to grab it.

She opened her eyes. "What—"

"It's just the phone. Go back to sleep," he told her, hoping to God it wasn't Griff changing his mind about him.

"Hello?" he murmured tentatively.

"Harry, it's Mike. I know we had this conversation earlier, but I think you should come out to the ranch for Thanksgiving dinner like you always do. It makes no sense—"

"Okay," Harry said calmly, stopping Mike's argument.

Mike remained silent for a moment, then said, "You agree?"

"I sure do."

"What changed your mind?"

Harry looked down at the woman in his bed, the one who'd just driven him wild with her lovemaking. "Let's just say I saw the light."

He clicked off the phone then and wrapped her in his arms, ready to go back to sleep. But Melissa stirred, asking sleepily, "Who was that?"

"Mike. He wanted to make sure I came to Thanksgiving dinner at the ranch. I told him I'd be there."

As if spurred, Melissa jumped up. "I forgot to tell you. Sorry, but I had other things on my mind last night." She wiggled her brows and grinned. "I saw

Mike and Caroline's house and I loved it. Dad offered to buy it for me if I'd stay here, and I took him up on the offer."

"He doesn't have to do that. I—"

She put a finger on his lips, silencing him. "He deserves to pay, Harry. He was trying to pressure me to stay."

"But that's because you told him you were leaving."

"Yes, but he should've had faith that I'd make the right decision on my own."

Harry knew this was an argument he wasn't going to win. But he still wasn't happy with Griff buying the house he was going to live in. "I can buy the house, Melissa."

"But it's Dad's wedding present to us. You can't say no to a present."

He had a feeling he'd never be able to say no to her, either. "Seems a rather extravagant gift," he muttered.

"Maybe," she said as she stroked his chest, "but I'm only going to get married once."

"You got that right." He watched her hand as it discovered his scar. As her palm slid lower on his torso, he felt himself become aroused. "I don't think I'm going to need that chocolate cake."

"Oh, really?" Melissa looked up at him, feigning innocence.

"You are a tease, Melissa Randall," Harry growled, capturing her hand.

"Yes, I am," she agreed as her lips met his.

Harry figured they'd save their dessert for another day. If he ever needed it at all.

Epilogue

Jake Randall stood up at the head of the table and asked the blessing for their Thanksgiving Day dinner. Several golden-brown turkeys, as well as bowls of potatoes, vegetables and homemade breads, weighted down the table, all made by Red and Mildred, who at their advanced age still prided themselves on how well they took care of the Randall clan.

And all the clan was there. The four brothers, their children, the cousins. As Jake said grace, he counted each of them as a blessing.

When he sat down, Griff called for everyone's attention. "Seems we've got even more to be thankful for," he said, smiling at his wife, who was seated next to him. "Camille's tests all came back benign." He bent to kiss her as the family cheered.

Across from him, Harry hugged Melissa. He knew how worried she'd been about her mother. Then he asked Jake and everyone seated at the table, "I know y'all can't wait to eat, but would you mind if I said something, too?"

Jake spoke for the family. "Of course not, Harry. Go ahead."

He stood up. "Well, you know this is my fourth year as a guest at your Thanksgiving table, but I want to tell you that I won't be coming as a guest anymore." He paused for a moment before he added, "Next time I'll be coming as a member of the famous Randall family." He smiled down at Melissa. "Melissa has agreed to marry me. The wedding is Sunday and you're all invited."

Dinner forgotten, everyone rushed to congratulate Harry and Melissa. All the women offered to help Camille with the reception. Then Jake said, "But I thought Melissa was going back to France."

"Only to pack up," Harry explained. "And I'll be going with her, for our honeymoon. We'll be back before Christmas, so if you have any shopping requests, let Melissa know."

"I'm opening my own jewelery design business based right here in Rawhide," she told everyone. "But I'll appreciate it if you'll all pitch in and make Harry feel at home when I have to be out of town."

There were a lot more questions, but Red and Mildred insisted everyone start eating before the food got cold.

As Harry feasted on the holiday spread, he looked around the table at the family he'd acquired overnight. The Randalls could be overwhelming, meddling, matchmaking, but no one could argue about how they loved each other. They were so different from his own family. He couldn't have given his future children a better gift than making them a part of this clan.

Harry wondered then if he should bite the bullet and get in touch with his parents and sister, to tell them about the wedding. He hadn't spoken to any of them in years. But somehow sitting there with all the Randalls, Harry knew he would. His parents could never be like Griff and Camille, but he'd have to accept whatever it was they could offer. Even for just a day. After all, as Melissa had said, he was only getting married once.

Melissa shook his arm, drawing him out of his deep thoughts. "Harry, did you hear all the wedding presents everyone wants to give us?" She listed the items.

"They can't give us all that," he whispered to her.

"Why not, Harry? That's the way we Randalls do things. You'd better get used to it."

"Give him time," Griff said from across the table. "He'll come 'round."

Then Jake offered to pay for the trip to Paris, and Harry couldn't rein in a protest. "I'm supposed to pay for the honeymoon. I know that much at least."

Jake just grinned at him.

Melissa put a comforting hand on his. "I can't tell Uncle Jake what to do. Can you?"

"N-no," he stammered. "But your dad will tell him."

Melissa just laughed at him. "Don't worry, Harry. They won't pay our bills after we're married. That'll be your job." She kissed him and everyone hooted.

When he pulled her close and deepened the kiss,

Griff teased, "There they go again. Kissing in front of everyone." But he couldn't be happier.

Melissa smiled at her husband-to-be. "We're going to have a lovely life together, Harry. I love you so much."

"I love you, too. And I promise—right here in front of everyone—that I'll do whatever it takes to make you happy."

"It just takes being yourself. You're the perfect man for me."

Harry's gaze scanned all the Randalls, his new family, then lit on his future wife. He wrapped his arm around her. "We've got a lot to be to be thankful for."

* * * * *

Watch for a heartwarming new miniseries—
DALLAS DUETS—by Judy Christenberry,
beginning with
DADDY NEXT DOOR,
coming January 2007,
only from Harlequin American Romance.

My husband could see beauty in a mud puddle. Literally. "Look at that, Louise," he'd say after a heavy spring rain. "Have you ever seen so many amazing colors in mud?"

I'd look and see nothing except brown, but he'd pick up a stick and swirl the mud till the colors of the earth emerged, and all of a sudden I'd see the world through his eyes—extraordinary instead of mundane.

Roy was my mirror to life. Four years ago when he died, it cracked wide open, and I've been living a smashed-up, sleepwalking life ever since.

If he were here on this balmy August night I'd be sailing with him instead of baking cheese straws in preparation for Tuesday-night quilting club with Patsy. I'd be striving for sex appeal in Bermuda shorts and bare-toed sandals instead of opting for comfort in walking shoes and a twill skirt with enough elastic around the waist to make allowances for two helpings of lemon-cream pie.

Not that I mind Patsy. Just the opposite. I love her. She's the only person besides Roy who creates wonder wherever she goes. (She creates mayhem, too, but we won't get into that.) She's my mirror now, as well as my compass.

Of course, I have my daughter, Diana, but I refuse to be the kind of mother who defines herself through her children. Besides, she has her own life now, a husband and a baby on the way.

I slide the last cheese straws into the oven and then go into my office and open e-mail.

From: "Miss Sass" <patsyleslie@hotmail.com>
To: "The Lady" <louisejernigan@yahoo.com>
Sent: Tuesday, August 15, 6:00 PM
Subject: Dangerous Tonight
Hey Lady,
I'm feeling dangerous tonight. Hot to trot, if you know what I mean. Or can you even remember?☺ Look out, bridge club, here I come. I'm liable to end up dancing on the tables instead of bidding three spades. Whose turn is it to drive, anyhow? Mine or thine?
XOXOX
Patsy
P.S. Lord, how did we end up in a club with no men?

This e-mail is typical "Patsy." She's the only person

I know who makes me laugh all the time. I guess that's why I e-mail her about ten times a day. She lives right next door, but e-mail satisfies my urge to be instantly and constantly in touch with her without having to interrupt the flow of my life. Sometimes we even save the good stuff for e-mail.

From: "The Lady" <louisejernigan@yahoo.com>
To: "Miss Sass" <patsyleslie@hotmail.com>
Sent: Tuesday, August 15, 6:10 PM
Subject: Re: Dangerous Tonight
So, what else is new, Miss Sass? You're always dangerous. If you had a weapon, you'd be lethal.☺
Hugs,
Louise
P.S. What's this about men? I thought you said your libido was dead?

I press Send then wait. Her reply is almost instantaneous.

From: "Miss Sass" <patsyleslie@hotmail.com>
To: "The Lady" <louisejernigan@yahoo.com>
Sent: Tuesday, August 15, 6:12 PM
Subject: Re: Dangerous Tonight
Ha! If I had a *brain* I'd be lethal.
And I said my libido was in hibernation, not DEAD!
Jeez, Louise!!!!!
P

Patsy loves to have the last word, so I shut off my computer.

* * * * *

*Want to find out what happens to their friendship
when Patsy and Louise both find the perfect man?*

*Don't miss
CONFESSIONS OF A NOT-SO-DEAD LIBIDO
by Peggy Webb,
coming to Harlequin NEXT
in November 2006.*

This holiday season, cozy up with

HARLEQUIN® *Romance*

 In November
we're proud to present

JUDY CHRISTENBERRY
Her Christmas Wedding Wish

A beautiful story of love and family found.

And

LINDA GOODNIGHT
Married Under The Mistletoe

Don't miss this installment of

The Brides of Bella Lucia

From the Heart. For the Heart.

www.eHarlequin.com

HRXMAS06

Introducing…

nocturne™

a dark and sexy new
paranormal romance line
from Silhouette Books.

USA TODAY bestselling author

LINDSAY McKENNA
UNFORGIVEN

KATHLEEN KORBEL
DANGEROUS TEMPTATION

*Launching October 2006,
wherever books are sold.*

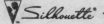